"So we're dealing with three guys with twinkling eyes?" Paige asked as she watched Piper continue flipping through the Book of Shadows. "Sounds like a bad fifties group. Somehow I doubt they'd be in there under that name."

"Did your guy give you a card, by any chance?" Phoebe asked.

"No," Paige said. "Just a flower. But he told me his name was Robin, if that helps."

"Robin?" Phoebe asked as she took the Book of Shadows from Piper. "As in Robin Goodfellow."

Paige's eyes went wide. "You don't mean—"

"I *knew* that quote was familiar," Phoebe interrupted. "The IT guy changed my column to read, 'Gentles, do not reprehend. If you pardon, I will mend.' It was from *A Midsummer Night's Dream*. We're not being stalked by a demon mob. If I'm not mistaken, we're all being bothered by the same guy. And even though we've never met him, I think we all know his name."

Even though Phoebe hadn't known what page to go to, she immediately landed on the entry she had been looking for.

Piper saw the page over her sister's shoulder and in an instant understood the identity of the demon. "Puck."

Charmed®

Published by Simon & Schuster

AS PUCK WOULD
HAVE IT

Charmed ®

AS PUCK WOULD HAVE IT

An original novel by Paul Ruditis

Based on the hit TV series created by

Constance M. Burge

SIMON SPOTLIGHT ENTERTAINMENT
New York   London   Toronto   Sydney

SSE

SIMON SPOTLIGHT ENTERTAINMENT
An imprint of Simon & Schuster Children's Publishing Division
1230 Avenue of the Americas, New York, New York 10020
® and © 2006 Spelling Television Inc. All Rights Reserved.
All rights reserved, including the right of reproduction in whole or in part in any form.
SIMON SPOTLIGHT ENTERTAINMENT and related logo are trademarks of Simon & Schuster, Inc.
Manufactured in the United States of America
First Edition 10 9 8 7 6 5 4 3 2 1
Library of Congress Control Number 2005933339
ISBN-13: 978-1-4169-1468-6
ISBN-10: 1-4169-1468-4

For Harry Gaskill

AS PUCK WOULD
HAVE IT

Prologue

San Diego, California

If there's one thing to be learned from a life that spans centuries, it's that evil doesn't keep to a schedule. While, to some, it may seem romantic to inspire death and destruction on the Witching Hour, or the Magic Hour, or even the Happy Hour, bad things are just as likely to happen on the half hour as well. The freaks did not just come out at night.

This was something that Puck had learned many, many years ago. Considering that some may have even called *him* one of the freaks, he knew full well that he could show up at any time of the day or night. But that knowledge didn't help him in his present situation. It didn't relieve the crick in his neck, the chill in his bones, or the numbness in his legs from sitting and waiting for so long in the brisk night air.

Sure, he could have conjured up any number of creature comforts for himself, but that wouldn't have been playing by the rules. Then again, since he was the one who made up the rules, why not just change them again? He would have to give that idea some serious thought if he was forced to wait much longer.

If only evil could learn to stick to a schedule.

He saw that the demon had finally decided to show up. Puck yawned and walked to the front gate as if he didn't have a care in the world. The casual observer would think little of the sight of a "man" out for a stroll in the middle of the night. Though one might question why he was trying to enter the zoo while it was closed—*that* part was a little strange.

Under normal circumstances the gate would pose little problem for the demon. Metal bars had long since ceased to be an issue, thanks to the collected strength he had amassed over the years. But metal bars weren't the only things protecting the animals on this night.

Shaking off the tingles of a leg that had fallen asleep, Puck easily leaped up to a nearby branch to get a better vantage point. He stood up on his perch above the gate and leaned forward to get a closer look at the demon. Even if the demon glanced in Puck's direction, he wouldn't see anything. Aside from the fact that the moonless night was pitch-black, Puck was currently invisible.

Not that Puck was afraid of being seen. The great and noble Puck—as his closest friends liked to call him—wasn't afraid of anything. He just didn't want to give himself away yet. It was going to be much more fun to watch the demon undetected. Puck was practically giddy with excitement as the demon approached the invisible barrier and slammed right into it.

This is the third time he's done that in the past two months, Puck thought. *When is he going to learn?*

The demon shook his head as if he wasn't sure what had just happened. Puck was tempted to add a cartoon sound effect to complement the move. He didn't seem to be a particularly bright demon, although the sweet deal he had set up for himself seemed to suggest otherwise. The demon tentatively held out a hand to find out what had stopped him. Again, this was something he had done on two other occasions.

Puck briefly considered removing the barrier to let the demon's hand pass through, then bringing it back up once the hand was on the other side, if only to see what would happen to the hand. But ultimately, Puck decided against it. Not that the cruelty of the action was the thing stopping him. That actually appealed to him. He was just afraid that he wouldn't be able to get the barrier back up in time.

The demon's hand made contact with the barrier, causing him to screw up his face in a perplexed look. Puck turned a huge spotlight on the demon so he could see the demon's reaction from his perch.

If the demon had been surprised when he hit the invisible barrier, it was nothing compared with how he reacted when he found himself in the hot spot of a klieg light.

"Who's there?" the demon shouted, holding a hand over his eyes to block the light.

"Good evening, kind sir," Puck said as he came into view within the glow of the spotlight. "What brings you out here on such a fine evening as this?"

"You!" the demon roared.

"Me?" Puck was shocked. "I don't recall issuing you an invitation. But I will certainly check with my social secretary."

"You!" the demon said again as he slammed into the barrier.

"Yes, my monosyllabic friend, we have already established that it is I, the merry wanderer of the night . . . the happy prankster of stage, screen, and literature . . . the one, the only . . . *Puck*!" he said, loving every minute of his introduction. He considered adding some canned applause, but decided that would be overkill. Sometimes Puck preferred a little subtlety.

"We have also established," Puck continued, "that there is a wall there that you are *just* not going to be able to get through. Does any of this seem even the least bit familiar? We have done this before, you know."

"What are you doing here, fairy?" The demon asked.

Puck's face fell into an evil glare as he reconsidered using the barrier to slice the demon in half. "Do not call me *fairy*," he growled.

Puck pushed out with his hands, sending a wave of power that slipped through the barrier and knocked the demon to the ground. If it had been any other demon, the blast would have sent him clear across the parking lot. Puck was actually surprised to see that it had blown the demon off his feet. This was not just any demon. This was a demon Puck had had several run-ins with before, and it was quite strong.

The demon wasn't down for long, though. In an instant he was up and running toward Puck. If there hadn't been an invisible barrier between the two of them, Puck would've been flattened.

To Puck's delight, the demon misjudged the distance as he slammed into the barrier again. Shaking it off quickly this time, he pounded his fists into the invisible barrier, trying to break through. Again, this was something he had done the other two times he had encountered similar barriers, and the result was no different.

The demon pounded with all his might—as well as the might of several other beings. He didn't even make a dent. Not that he could have seen said dent if he had managed to make one. The barrier was, after all, invisible.

Puck yawned again as he grew bored with the entire situation. It was considerably late— long after his bedtime—and he had a notoriously short attention span to begin with. The demon's reliance on previously failed tactics was just not keeping things interesting enough for Puck.

"You can't stop me, you know," the demon said, when he finally gave up on trying to break through the barrier.

"Seems like I've been pretty successful so far," Puck replied as he looked down on the demon, both literally and figuratively.

"You've delayed me, maybe," the demon said. "But you can't stop me for good."

Puck didn't have a witty comeback for that one. The demon was right. Puck could not stop him for good.

Puck could certainly make life difficult for the demon. He had already had plenty of fun doing just that over the past few weeks. But he knew that those games had ended, and the demon was about to take it to the next level.

"So what do you have to say to that, fairy?" the demon said, taunting Puck. "I don't hear you laughing now."

Puck quickly threw his arms forward again. This time, the blast did knock the demon up into the air, sending him into the koala bear section of the parking lot. It wasn't quite as far as the duck-billed platypus section, but Puck was satisfied.

He watched as the demon got to his feet. Apparently his nemesis had decided to give up for the evening. Instead of coming back for more, the demon just skulked off like a child who'd had his favorite toy taken away.

Puck hadn't enjoyed that exchange half as much as he had expected to. Probably because the demon had been right: Puck couldn't actually stop him. At least, he couldn't do it alone.

That realization brought a smile to his face. He knew what had to be done.

It was time for him to have some fun.

Chapter 1

San Francisco, California

"Okay, great," Piper said into the phone as she held it in the crook of her neck—she was lacking a free hand at the moment. Her son, Wyatt, was hanging on one arm while she was trying to sign for a package using the other. And at the same time she was trying to focus her attention on her slightly agitated assistant club manager over the phone.

"Put the shipment in the storeroom for now and I'll worry about it tomorrow," she said. "Yes, I am subscribing to the Scarlett O'Hara school of business management now. . . . Okay . . . thanks."

Piper had scaled back her responsibilities at her club, P3, since the birth of her son. The problem was that everyone who worked there seemed to think the place was going to crumble to the ground without her. It was nice to feel needed, but the current level of dependency exhibited by her staff made her infant child seem self-sufficient by comparison.

Piper pushed end on the cordless phone, finished scribbling her name on the delivery man's electronic pad, rested the phone on the package, and took it from him all while Wyatt continued to tug at her blouse.

"Thanks," she said to the delivery man without missing a step. Then she closed the front door, dropped the package on the side table, moved into the conservatory, and placed Wyatt in his playpen.

"Just another quiet morning in Halliwell Manor," Piper said to the handsome man in the blue jumpsuit standing in the conservatory.

Actually, she was speaking to the back of his head. The man was checking out the glass windows that made up the wall of the conservatory. She had left him a minute ago to answer the front door and was surprised to find that he was still working when she returned. She had thought the job was done. Apparently, he didn't like what he had seen because he pulled a small rag from his back pocket and started wiping the pane he was examining.

"Sorry if we're adding to the ruckus," the man said as he finished wiping down the window and took a sip from the glass of milk Piper had poured him before she answered the door. "Don't you just love that word? 'Ruckus'? Brings all kinds of images to mind, doesn't it?"

Piper's image of a "ruckus" wasn't all that pleasant. In fact, it was the reason the handsome gentleman was at her house this morning.

"No problem at all, Mr. Goode," Piper said. "Your crew has been amazing. I never imagined the place could get so clean in only a couple hours." Piper was still impressed that the crew had managed to come at 9 A.M. that morning, clean the entire first and second floors well enough to eliminate all remnants of what seemed like their thousandth demon attack, and leave the place looking totally spotless.

She wished that she had thought of calling a cleaning service before. It would have saved her and her sisters a lot of work over the years. Considering what a mess it was to stop the forces of evil, she'd probably be one of their best customers from now on.

"At Goode's Cleaning Service, we aim to please," Mr. Goode said as he pretended to tip his nonexistent hat to her. "Just to go over things, we've dusted, mopped, and vacuumed, cleaned the windows, polished the fixtures, and even managed to get that stubborn green sludge off the floor."

Piper noticed that the part about the green sludge was spoken with a bit of a question in his voice. She couldn't blame him. It was an unusual stain. The cleaning crew had made a similar remark when they first saw it.

"Cooking experiment gone horribly wrong," Piper said, trying to explain away the sludge. It had actually been all that was left of a Goo

Demon. She had cleaned up the goo herself before calling in the crew. There had been no easy way to explain the thick coating of gunk that had covered *everything* in the front hall the night before.

Goode didn't seem to be buying her explanation for the sludge, though. "A cooking experiment that leaves a stain on the living room floor?"

"When I get going, no room is safe," Piper said, trying to laugh the question off.

There was a brief pause as Mr. Goode mulled over her answer. It seemed like he believed her. Either that or he had decided to leave the crazy lady alone and move on. "So then, everything is to your satisfaction?"

"*Beyond*," Piper said. "You don't even know how much time you've saved me. I may even be able to take a nap along with Wyatt this afternoon."

Goode leaned over the baby's playpen, tickling the boy under the chin. "I'm just glad to help a mom out," he said. "Especially a working mom such as yourself. What is it you do?"

"I run a nightclub," she explained. "P3?"

"Never heard of it," Goode said. "But I don't get out much. I'm a homebody. An exciting night for me is when TLC runs a *Clean Sweep* marathon. I can watch those people clean houses for hours."

"Well . . . okay," Piper said.

"But I imagine running a nightclub can get fairly busy," he added.

"You don't know the half of it," Piper said, meaning far more than she was saying. It was true that P3 took up an inordinate amount of time, but that wasn't the only job she had.

"I'm sure I don't," Goode replied with a cryptic smile. "I can imagine having a young child around the house must keep you very busy too."

"Particularly this one," Piper said, remembering how Wyatt had managed to orb into her arms in the middle of the Goo Demon's attack. Luckily, his force field protected him, and Piper, from harm. "He can be a handful."

"Something all mothers think about their children," Goode replied as he put his now empty glass of milk down on a coaster on the table. "I meet a lot of people in my business. You know, I'm in and out of a lot of homes. It seems like everyone's busy these days. Too busy to relax and enjoy life."

"Well, you've saved me from a full day of cleaning," Piper said. "What do I owe you?"

"Oh, money won't be necessary," Goode said. "I have no use for it, really. All that worthless paper lying about. But . . . that is a lovely blouse."

"Thank you," Piper said uncertainly. She was wearing a black embroidered V-neck top with long sleeves, something Phoebe had gotten her for her last birthday. It was one of her most comfortable tops, but certainly nothing special—just something she wore around the house.

"I can pay with a check, if you don't want cash," Piper said, going for her checkbook, despite the man's strange comments. "You never did give me an estimate."

"I wasn't sure what the job would cost until it was done," Goode explained. "But I think that blouse will do fine."

"I'm sorry?"

"Your blouse," he said. "It should be a sufficient fee."

Piper's eyes went wide as she stepped away from the man. She held her hands up in case it became necessary to freeze him. At least his crew had gone home already. She would have been more concerned if his entire team were in the house with him. Although if they had been around, he might not have made his crazy request.

"You want me to take off my shirt for you?" Piper asked, making sure there wasn't a misunderstanding.

"Heavens no." Goode laughed. "You can go upstairs to change. I'm not asking for a peep show or anything like that. I just think your shirt would be fair compensation for a job well done. If you think it's too much, I have a spare pair of socks I could give as change. I don't usually give that kind of discount to first-time clients, but you strike me as an honorable woman."

Piper looked down at Wyatt. She slid herself

between Mr. Goode and the baby, just in case. This interaction was bizarre on so many levels. The man was literally asking for the shirt off her back. She figured it was pointless to explain that it probably didn't come close in value to the amount of work his crew had put into cleaning the place. Aside from the fact that it was a ridiculous brand of logic, she was not about to give him her blouse.

"I'm sorry, Mr. Goode, but I'm not comfortable paying you in clothing," Piper said, holding up her checkbook. "I'm sure we can work out a reasonable price."

At this point she was willing to pay any amount just to get the freak out of her house. It wasn't like Goode's Cleaning Service had come to her on a recommendation from someone in the magical realm. She wouldn't have been so surprised about the request if it had come from someone her deceased Grams had recommended. Heck, Piper would have almost expected some odd arrangement to be made, in that case. After all, the fairy tales about giving away a newborn child in exchange for spinning straw into gold had to come from somewhere. But this was totally unexpected—Piper had found Goode's Cleaning Service listed in the Yellow Pages, not some book from the Underworld.

"Then we seem to have reached an impasse," Goode said. The jovial tone had left his voice, and his face had turned from bright and smiling to dark and brooding. Piper could have sworn his light blue eyes had turned darker as well.

"I think you should leave," Piper said, trying to put more distance between him and her son. There was no telling what a man like this would do. Her hands tensed at her sides, ready to stop time on a moment's notice if it became necessary.

"But I have performed a service for you," Goode said as if he was asking for the most logical thing in the world. "It is only fair that I be compensated. I have been doing this for many, many years, young lady, and this is the first time I have ever had anyone refuse to pay my fee."

"I *have* offered to pay you for your work," Piper said, trying to remain calm. She didn't know where he got off calling her "young lady" since, as far as she could tell, they seemed to be the same age. "I can't help it if you won't accept my money."

"Do not insult me with your worthless paper," Goode said. He was now being entirely unreasonable. "If that's how you want to be, then I shall take back my services."

Piper looked around the conservatory. It was sparkling clean. She wasn't quite sure what he meant by "take back my services," but it sounded ominous.

Goode walked over to the tallest of the potted plants and touched one of its leaves. "You have one more chance," he said simply. "Give me the shirt."

"No."

"Don't say I didn't warn you."

Goode gave the plant a good push. Piper watched as the plant fell over, spilling dirt onto the floor. The top of the tree banged into a wicker chair, sending it sliding across the floor and smacking into the wall, knocking a picture off its hook. On the way down, the picture knocked over a vase, which tipped on its side and rolled into the dining room.

Piper listened from where she stood in the conservatory as the crashing and banging continued from room to room throughout the first floor. She couldn't even bring herself to look as the damage added up to far more than it would have cost to replace one slightly worn blouse. However, she couldn't ignore the TV stand as it rolled out of the living room and into the hall, disappearing behind the wall.

The path of destruction finally ended when Piper heard what she thought sounded like the television crashing into the grandfather clock.

"What are you, insane?" Piper asked, furious.

"Next time, I expect you'll be more willing to pay your debts," Mr. Goode said as he turned from Piper and walked toward the foyer.

"Wait just a second," Piper said as she followed Goode, stepping over the fallen plant.

The man did not stop. He just kept walking to the door as if she wasn't there.

"I said, wait." Piper threw her hands up, stopping time.

But Goode kept walking.

At first Piper thought her powers had malfunctioned. It wouldn't have been the first time something like that had happened. But she noticed a picture that had been swinging on the edge of its hook had frozen in place. She looked back at the broken grandfather clock and saw that the second hand wasn't moving either. *Though that could have more to do with the minor destruction to the place than magic,* she thought.

Either way, Goode had been unaffected by her magic. He stormed out the front door and slammed it shut behind him.

When Piper unfroze time, the picture that had been swinging came crashing to the floor—a final punctuation mark on the odd scene.

Piper considered going after the man—if he was even a man. The fact that he hadn't stopped when she froze time meant that he was a very powerful being, probably an Upper-Level Demon. But what would an Upper-Level Demon be doing cleaning her house? And why would he want her clothes?

As she surveyed the devastation on the first floor, she knew without a shadow of a doubt that she would have a chance to ask him in the near future. A new blouse couldn't have been all that he was after.

He would most definitely be back.

Chapter 2

" . . . **And finally,** I hate to resort to a twenty-first-century cliché, but he's just not that into you."

Phoebe Halliwell checked over her latest advice column for the *Bay Mirror*. Everything looked fine, so far. Having written this same column three times previously, she didn't question any of the actual advice. At this point, she had no doubt that she was telling her readers the right thing to do.

The spelling was fine, and the sentence structure worked for her. She hated ending on an overused cliché, but every now and then the folks in Market Research insisted that she throw in a trendy pop culture reference to "keep it fresh."

This bothered Phoebe immensely, but she went along with the decree. Her editor, Elise, had been having a hard time adjusting to the new regime brought in under new head honcho Jason Dean. The recent crop of MFA program graduates had been urging Elise to target the paper to a younger demographic. The problem was that that demographic would much rather get their news online, if they were actually interested in the news at all.

Since the paper couldn't do anything to make the news itself "hipper" and "more youth-friendly" (other words that appeared in the "keep it fresh" memo), the advice column, "Ask Phoebe," was one of the chosen focal points for bringing in the coveted eighteen-to-thirty-four-year-olds. That meant people in several departments were going over every word that she wrote, adding their own comments and questions, and sending the copy back to her. She was getting used to finding copies of her column marked up with purple pen in her in-box, as if these people didn't know that editorial corrections were traditionally done in red.

For Elise's sake, this was one battle Phoebe chose not to fight . . . for the time being, at least.

Phoebe maneuvered her mouse to activate the pull-down menu at the top left of her screen. She clicked on save. But as soon as she released the left button on her mouse, the screen went black and the computer shut down.

"AAAAAHHH!" she yelled in frustration, lifting the laptop as if she were about to fling it across the room.

"You break it, you bought it," Elise said as she entered Phoebe's office.

Phoebe put the computer back down on her desk. She hadn't really been planning to throw it, but the idea was certainly tempting. It was a small price to pay for venting her frustration.

"If you want my column in by the deadline, I'm going to have to do it on another computer," Phoebe said. "Mine has been acting up recently. Any chance you'll let me borrow yours for a few minutes?"

"That's fine," Elise said, "but technically we're already past deadline. What has IT said about the problem?"

"They said someone will be here in an hour," Phoebe replied.

"They couldn't help you over the phone?" Elise asked.

"No." Phoebe sighed. "It's insane. I can send e-mails, balance my checkbook, and even type notes for that book I'm thinking of writing someday. But every time I try to write my column, the computer shuts down. And when I get it back up, the column's gone. It can't even be recovered."

"Maybe I shouldn't let you borrow my computer," Elise joked. "It sounds like the problem is your advice, not flawed technology."

"Thanks. You're a great help," Phoebe said as she looked for a notepad in her desk. This time she was going to write her column out in longhand before it disappeared into cyberspace. At least then she wouldn't have to keep racking her brain to remember exactly what she had written.

"Go use one of the computers in the bullpen," Elise said. "See if that . . . hello."

That was a non sequitur, Phoebe thought as she continued to riffle through her desk drawer.

Phoebe looked up and saw a very handsome blond man dressed in chinos, a pink dress shirt, and a light blue tie standing in the doorway. Even from her seat across the room, she could see he had the most intriguingly gray eyes that she had ever seen. She understood why Elise had stopped mid-sentence.

"Hello, indeed," Phoebe mumbled.

"Ms. Halliwell?" the man asked from the doorway.

"That'd be her," Elise said as she turned her attention back to Phoebe. "Let me know when your column's ready or we're going to have to go with one of those 'The Best of Phoebe' reissues I keep around for when another family emergency comes up and you blow a deadline."

Phoebe saw that Elise was smiling, but she knew that her editor had gotten her point across.

She wasn't surprised to hear that Elise had articles in reserve. Considering the number of demons that interfered with Phoebe's work schedule, she did miss her deadlines with surprising frequency. But she always managed to get her work in *close* to on time. Or at least before the paper went to press.

"I'll do what I can," Phoebe said as Elise left her office. She then directed her attention to the man in the doorway. "Can I help you?" she asked.

"I think the better question is, can *I* help *you*?" the man replied.

Phoebe's mind was full of retorts. None of which was appropriate for an office setting. Not that that had ever stopped her in the past—she was currently involved with her boss's boss . . . sort of.

"And you are?" she asked.

"Robert Fellows," the man said. "From IT."

Phoebe's interest was definitely piqued. *Not only is this guy hot*, she thought, *but he's potentially my savior.*

Even with Jason out of the country again, getting her computer fixed trumped flirtation. At least, for the moment.

"Oh, thank you," Phoebe said with relief as she got out of her seat to give him clear access to her laptop. "My computer has been acting crazy for days."

"Have you considered that it might not be acting?" Robert asked as he moved around her desk to the computer. "Computer insanity is a serious condition."

"Maybe I should write a column about it," Phoebe replied.

"And take a break from advising the lovelorn?" Robert asked. "That might not be a bad idea."

"You read my column?" Phoebe asked, ignoring the implied insult. She just assumed that what he had meant to say had come out wrong.

It always amazed her that people actually voluntarily read anything she wrote. She kept expecting Elise to come into her office one day and tell her it was all a joke; that they only needed something to fill the space before people turned to the comics, or that they had decided to dump her column so they could run more ads. It was always a pleasant surprise when someone stopped her to tell her they had read it.

"I've been known to peruse it from time to time," Robert said as he sat and looked at the clipboard he had carried in with him. "According to your ticket, the computer keeps shutting down while you work?"

"Every time I'm writing my column," Phoebe confirmed as Robert started tapping on the keys.

"Maybe your computer doesn't like the advice you've been giving."

Phoebe laughed at the joke, but stopped herself mid-giggle. Aside from the fact that he was the second person to make that joke in the past few minutes, she noticed that the playful tone had been missing from Robert's voice. For a moment, she wondered if he was being serious. He *had* said something about the computer actually being crazy just a moment ago.

"Somehow, I don't think my computer is that sensitive," she said.

"I do know that it couldn't possibly be as sensitive as you think your readership is," Robert said. "You do kind of coddle them."

"I don't cod—"

"Like that woman in your last column," he continued. The tone was back to being light-hearted, but now the subject matter wasn't matching the mood. "The one with the boyfriend who was bad about returning her calls. You told her to dump him."

"It wasn't just about the phone calls," Phoebe said. "There were other things too. I suggested that she get out of the relationship before she got hurt."

"Exactly!" Robert said as he rebooted the computer.

"'Exactly' *what*?" Phoebe asked. "I stand by that advice."

"But where's the fun in that?" Robert asked. "Things don't get interesting until real feelings are involved." He got up from her chair. "I need you to type in your password."

Phoebe paused for a moment, not sure what to do. The man was obviously insulting her, but in the most insane way possible. Like she was actually going to advise people to get hurt. She decided to ignore the debate and instead try to get her computer fixed quickly so the guy would leave.

Phoebe sat down in front of her computer and typed in her latest password. She changed it a couple times a month. Right now, she was going through lists of demons she had vanquished. She typed in "Kurzon" and waited.

"I spared the woman from getting hurt," Phoebe said, somewhat surprised by the fact that she couldn't let the matter drop. "That's why she wrote to me for advice in the first place."

"Sure, if you want to take the easy way," Robert said. "But if she's not properly hurt, how is anyone going to help her seek revenge on the louse? You do know he's cheating on her with her best friend, right?"

Phoebe forgot her computer for the moment. "Do you know these people?" she asked. That would explain why he seemed to be taking the advice so personally. Or maybe he was in a similar situation where he was the cheating boyfriend.

"Let's just say I know the *type*," he replied with a wave as if that part was unimportant. "So now she's going to dump him. He'll move on to the best friend full-time, acting like the relationship is new and she was there to pick up the pieces. The girlfriend will blame her best friend for taking his side, but she'll never really know that he was playing her all along. Then she'll never feel the need to get back at him. And he'll never learn his lesson."

"But, again," Phoebe insisted, "she won't get hurt."

"That's exactly my point," Robert said. "If she doesn't get hurt, then he'll never get hurt. And how is he supposed to get what he deserves?"

Phoebe was dumbfounded. She wasn't sure, but she thought her mouth may have been hanging open.

"Well, if you need anything else"—he placed his business card on the desk beside her computer—"you can call me at this number. It was nice chatting with you."

Robert was out the door before she could respond. She didn't even bother to look at the card. She was still in shock over the fact that he had just suggested she should advise people to let themselves be hurt so they could hurt others. Her Market Research department would just *love* that. Legal would probably be just as thrilled.

Phoebe tried to shake off the encounter and get back to work. She was on a deadline, after all.

Past it, actually, she thought.

This time, she was pleased to see that the computer had actually managed to save a copy of her column. She clicked on the recovered document and scanned through it to give the piece one last edit and make sure everything had survived the latest crash.

As soon as she saw the first response, she knew that something was seriously wrong. She continued reading the other responses, growing more concerned that it wasn't just some bizarre glitch. It would have been impossible for the computer to just arbitrarily do what it had done.

Every single one of her answers had been

changed. No matter what the question, every answer had the same short response:

Gentles, do not reprehend. If you pardon, I will mend.

The phrase seemed vaguely familiar to Phoebe. It was something she had stumbled across in the past. But that wasn't her focus, at the moment. The words themselves weren't the problem.

There was only one possible explanation: Robert had gone in and changed everything. But there was no way he could have done it so quickly. Unless he had been the one who had messed up the computer in the first place. . . .

Maybe she had given him bad advice and this was his payback. Or maybe she had given advice to his ex-girlfriend and it had resulted in her breaking up with him. In any case, his behavior was inappropriate and entirely unprofessional.

Phoebe picked up his business card. He probably wasn't back at his desk yet, but she was fine with leaving him a message. She planned to give him—and his superiors—a piece of her mind.

As soon as her fingers touched the card, Phoebe heard the sound of a trumpet blaring in her ears. She recoiled from the shock of the sound. As she looked out into the bullpen, she realized that no one else had reacted. She was the only one who had heard the noise. It was perfectly normal for Phoebe to get a premonition when she touched something. That had been happening for years. But this time, she didn't see any images from the future or from the past. She had only heard a trumpet, playing a long, shrill note.

Phoebe forgot all about her computer as she wondered what the sound had meant.

Chapter 3

Paige closed her eyes for a moment and basked in the wonderful silence of the forest around her. A slight breeze rustled through the trees and caressed her face, adding to the peaceful setting. This was the most relaxed she had felt in a while. Opening her eyes again, she continued along the path through the tall trees, listening to the hushed sounds all around her.

She had needed to have a relaxing weekend for a long time. It seemed like she had been fighting demons nonstop lately. In fact, a demon had almost forced her to cancel the trip altogether. Goulahga—whom her sisters had nicknamed the Goo Demon—had almost destroyed the Manor just one day earlier. Paige was still finding ecto-plasmic residue in her hair, even though she had taken an hour-long shower the night before.

The fact that Goulahga had nearly killed her before she could find all the ingredients for the vanquishing potion only made this getaway all the more important. It wasn't her fault that she hadn't known that adder's-tongue and the dog-tooth violet were the same healing herb. She needed to find a better connection with nature if she was going to continue to serve it without dying in the process. And facing one's own mortality helped put things in perspective.

Paige still considered herself new to this magic business, and it wasn't just because her sisters had three years on her when it came to knowing about their abilities. Some of the more evil beings the Charmed Ones encountered were hundreds of years old. Even for powerful witches like themselves, that was a lot of knowledge to go up against.

When Paige had first suggested a weekend away to clear their heads, she hadn't really expected her sisters to take her up on it. Piper had way too many responsibilities between her family and P3. Going camping for a weekend wasn't exactly easy to do with a baby in the house. Phoebe had been pretty busy lately, too, since her column was taking off. She was becoming a fixture on the San Francisco media scene. In addition to writing her column, she had public appearances to make, and other business-related events to attend. So Paige wasn't surprised when her sisters begged off and suggested that she go alone. And frankly, she was a bit relieved.

Of course, Piper and Phoebe had mentioned

that the offer would have been more tempting if Paige had planned a weekend at a five-star hotel. Preferably one with a pool, spa, and in-room babysitting service. But Paige wanted to reconnect with the earth. She wanted to get in touch with the natural magic that was all around her. Sitting in a concrete pool filled with highly chlorinated water wasn't exactly her idea of communing with nature. She couldn't think of a better way than camping.

Paige had orbed to the edge of the forest an hour earlier. She probably could have kept orbing around until she found the perfect campsite, but she preferred to hike. It would have been contradictory to her plan to go orbing all over the forest until she found a comfortable spot.

Phoebe had been kind enough to buy her a small GPS device to make up for the fact that Paige was taking the trip on her own. Paige had graciously accepted the present, but she didn't intend to use it. That, too, would have negated the whole purpose of the weekend.

At the end of her first hour in the forest, Paige decided she could use a short rest. She saw a small clearing off the well-trodden path. It was far enough from the main trail that she wouldn't be disturbed.

She entered the clearing and was happy to discover that it was as close to a perfect circle as she was going to find in nature. It wasn't a good spot to camp; it was a little overgrown, and

rocks jutted up through the dirt at various inter-
vals, but it would serve for a short break. She
even managed to find a nice patch of grass
directly in the center.

Paige dropped the backpack containing her
tent and other necessities for the weekend on the
ground, and took a seat on the soft grass. She
crossed her legs, took a deep, cleansing breath,
and closed her eyes. The silence was more pronounced here than on the trail. Paige slowed her
breathing as she concentrated on picking out the
sounds of nature in the quiet around her.

Using meditation techniques she had learned
from a book Piper had found for her, Paige was
able to hear things that she suspected most hik-
ers could not. Squirrels and chipmunks were
scampering through the brush. Birds were wing-
ing their way through the tall trees above her,
and if she concentrated, she could hear their
wings flapping. There was water rushing, far off
in the distance. It seemed to be coming from the
north, which meant she might find a good place
to camp in that direction.

So much for needing the GPS, she thought.

Paige focused on the sounds of the birds.
Connecting with animals was something that
most witches could do. Paige herself had felt like
she understood her friends' pets when she was
growing up. At the time, she had chalked it up to
an overactive imagination, but now she wasn't
too sure. She hoped to be able to tap into that part

of her inner self this weekend, figuring it would be easier to start with something small, like a sparrow.

She could hear chirping directly overhead. One of the birds had landed nearby. Paige wondered if the bird had felt her presence and come to investigate, or if it had just gotten tired and needed a place to rest. Paige tried to open her mind to the bird. She wasn't sure what it was supposed to feel like, but she concentrated as hard as she could.

Nothing happened.

Paige decided to try a different route. She remembered what she had read in the Book of Shadows about contacting a spirit-guide. The process required some preparation of the area first, but Paige would try that part later. For now, she wanted to get a feel for her guide, not necessarily meet the animal.

As Paige's mind concentrated on the ritual to contact a spirit-guide, she heard a more human variety of creature approaching. It scared her a bit that the person had been able to get so close before she had heard anything. She'd been so focused on connecting with the bird that she hadn't heard anyone coming in the distance. She silently tried to wish the person away. She didn't want to be disturbed.

Paige briefly considered trying a glamour to make herself blend in with the forest surroundings, but that kind of magic was a bit more advanced than what she usually practiced. As she heard the footsteps grow closer, she simply hoped that the person approaching would see that she wanted to be alone and continue on his or her merry way.

The footsteps stopped somewhere around the edge of the clearing. Paige waited for the person to either speak or walk away, but neither happened. The person just stood there, staring at her. Even with her eyes closed, she was sure she could feel the stranger's glare. Aside from being rude, it was beginning to get a little unnerving.

Paige risked a glance. She saw an auburn-haired man standing off to the side of the clearing. She was relieved to find that he wasn't staring at her. His attention was focused on the tree beside him. She couldn't see what he was doing, but she had a fairly good idea. He had been looking for a spot off the path to relieve himself.

Paige let out a soft cough to let him know someone was behind him. She could tell that he was startled as he finished his business. He turned to Paige, blushing. When she got a full-on look at his face, she lost her connection with nature completely. He was jarringly handsome.

"Um . . . hi," the man said. "I didn't realize someone was out here."

"I kind of figured," Paige said from her seated position on the ground.

"Taking a rest?" he asked.

"Sort of," Paige replied. "Meditation."

"Here?" he asked, checking out the area skeptically. Suddenly it seemed much rockier and more uncomfortable than it had when she had first sat down.

"All I need is silence," she said.

"This is fine for that," he said, considering. "But if you really want to get in touch with nature, I know the perfect place."

Paige looked at the handsome stranger for a moment. It wasn't exactly safe to go off with unfamiliar men she met in the middle of the woods. But if anything happened, she could always orb a boulder over his head and drop it on him. Of course, she'd only use that as a last resort. "What did you have in mind?" she asked innocently as she stood.

"It's just a short hike," he said, pointing through the trees in a direction that was definitely off the beaten path. Paige noticed that he wanted them to head north, in the direction of the rushing water she had heard during her brief meditation.

Paige silently debated the offer in her mind. She would be crazy to go walking with a stranger, but he seemed fairly harmless. Besides, she had just begun to invoke a spirit-guide when she had found him. She hadn't expected to receive such a literal response, but who was she to question the powers-that-be.

Then again, considering her history with the

powers-that-be, it was a pretty wise choice to question them. But that was neither here nor there.

"I'm Paige," she said, holding out a hand in greeting.

"Robin," he said as he started to put out his hand. Before she could take it, he quickly pulled his hand away as if he had just realized something. Smiling shyly, he took a small bottle of hand-sanitizing lotion from his pack. He quickly poured some out and rubbed it into his hands.

Paige gave an uncomfortable laugh, then nodded with appreciation over his cleanliness.

"As I was saying"—he took her hand—"My name is Robin. And it will be my pleasure to be your guide."

"The pleasure is all mine," Paige said.

"But, first"—he waved his hands in front of her eyes and produced a flower, seemingly from out of nowhere—"a lovely bloom for the lovely lady."

Robin held the flower up to Paige's face. It was pink and purple and looked like an orchid, yet unlike any orchid she had ever seen. She breathed in the scent, which was also unique. It was a delightful combination of jasmine and mixed spices.

Robin placed the flower in her hair, sliding it behind her ear.

"Impressed by my magic?" he asked.

Paige found his question charming for a slew of reasons she could not explain to him. "I am in awe of your power," she said, playing along.

A quick scan of the area revealed there were no similar flowers around. Either he routinely carried a flower with him for just such occasions— which was a creepy thought—or he did possess more impressive magic than a simple sleight of hand. As they left the clearing, Paige tried to shake the suspicion from her mind. He had probably just found the interesting bloom earlier and picked it up for himself. It was only a lucky break that he had found someone to share it with. At least, that's what she tried to convince herself. She couldn't truly embrace the idea.

"So," Paige said. "Are you a nature lover?"

"You mean am I enchanted with it?" Robin asked. "Some might say so."

"I thought we were speaking seriously," Paige said.

"No, I think *you* were speaking seriously," Robin replied as he held back a branch so Paige could pass through. "I rarely speak seriously."

"I'm picking up on that," Paige said.

They had come to a large fallen tree trunk. Robin quickly hopped up on it and held a hand down to Paige.

"Are you sure you know where you're going?" Paige asked as she eyed the rotting tree skeptically.

"Know where I'm going?" Robin said, motioning for Paige to take his hand. "I thought I was following you."

Paige grabbed his hand and let him pull her up on the tree trunk. Luckily the wood held. They jumped down on the other side and continued along what Paige would barely identify as a trail.

The banter continued as they followed the overgrown path around a hill, where the forest opened up on the edge of a precipice. They were standing about a hundred feet above a rushing river and looking out over the picturesque setting of a small valley. There was a sizable break before the tree line, and as she looked down, Paige thought that it would make for the perfect camp spot if only there were a way to get down there.

She figured she could have orbed there if Robin hadn't been with her. Then again, he surely didn't think that she was about to spend the weekend camping with him. A hike together was one thing. Paige wasn't about to let the stranger sleep in a tent right next to hers. But since he had brought her there specifically for meditation, she figured she could just wait him out, then orb down to the campsite on her own.

Paige looked down longingly at the valley. The trees surrounded a clearing in a semi-circle. From the distance, she could make out a bed of flowers. She noticed that the colors looked similar to the bloom in her hair. *Interesting,* she thought. *I wonder if he climbed all the way up here.*

If there was ever a setting for a fairy tale, this

would have been it, Paige silently mused. *Complete with a witch.*

"It's beautiful," Paige finally said, admiring the view.

"Fresh air, pure earth, rushing water," Robin said with a snap of his fingers that lit a small flame on his thumb. "And a little fire to complete the elements. The perfect spot for meditation."

"Or to start a forest fire," Paige said, blowing on his thumb to put out the flame. The magic tricks were cute, but there was something about this setup that was starting to bother Paige. Robin was just a little too in tune with what she was looking for, and his "tricks" were just a little too real. It wasn't lost on her that he had effectively walked her to the edge of a cliff, either.

"Here, let me get that for you," Robin said as he grabbed at her pack.

"That's okay," Paige said as she tried to step away.

"Nonsense," Robin said as he slipped it off her back. "You can't very well get in touch with nature with a heavy backpack strapped to you. I'm guessing it's got your cell phone, a digital camera, and maybe even an iPod inside. None of that is going to help you with your meditation.

"Here," he continued. "Why don't I just take care of these distractions for you."

Before Paige could even ask what he meant, Robin threw her backpack over the ledge and down into the river below. For a moment she could do nothing but blink in surprise at the total audacity of her so-called guide.

Once Paige regained her senses, she considered orbing the pack back up to her, but then realized that it was already lost. She'd barely had the chance to debate the risk of revealing her abilities before her belongings had been whisked away in the rushing water.

"What the hell did you do that for?" Paige asked as she moved toward the man, threateningly.

"I was just trying to help," Robin said as he backed away.

"Help?" Paige asked. "By throwing all my possessions into the river."

"A wise man once said we will never truly find our inner selves until we divest our outer selves of our worldly possessions," he said as he continued to retreat. "Of course, the man who said that was me, so you might have a different opinion on how wise the man is."

"You are insane," Paige said. "I can't believe—" But she couldn't finish her sentence. She had just realized that Robin had backed himself right over the edge of the precipice. But instead of falling, he was hovering in midair.

Robin seemed to realize this as well as he looked down at the empty air beneath his feet and then back up at Paige. He smiled broadly at her with a twinkle in his green eyes. "Well, look at that," he said.

"Who are you?" Paige asked, throwing up her hands defensively, ready to orb herself out of the area if necessary.

"Now there's an interesting question," Robin said. "Who is any of us? I leave you to ponder that transcendental thought."

Without another word, he disappeared. And although he was no longer present, Paige could hear laughter echoing through the valley with a "Ho, ho, ho."

Chapter 4

Piper flipped through the Book of Shadows growing angrier with each passing page. She had put Wyatt in his crib an hour ago, before she'd started cleaning up the broken glass from the bizarre "cleaning" incident. The last thing she needed was for the baby to cut himself on remnants of that morning's disaster.

She had picked up all of the sharp objects, but left the fallen pictures, toppled chairs, and everything else as it was. There would be time for a more thorough cleaning later. As long as the first floor was baby-proofed, she was free to look into who—or *what*—was messing with her.

It was ridiculous that she was cleaning up the house after the cleaning crew had come and gone. At least she wasn't out any money. She could still hire another cleaning crew to get rid of the new mess, but she was understandably reluctant to make another call. The Yellow Pages just wasn't the reliable source it had been in the past.

In hindsight, Piper should have just given Mr. Goode her shirt, if only to get rid of him. *But how was I supposed to know the freak would destroy the house?*

So far, the Book of Shadows hadn't been much help in the area of magic cleaning services, but her anger was helping fuel her research. She'd go through the tome as many times as it took until she found a clue about the inappropriately named Mr. Goode.

"Piper!" Phoebe yelled from the first floor. The yell was followed by the sound of the front door slamming. It looked like Piper wasn't the only one having a rough morning. Something must have happened for Phoebe to come barging into the house like that. Especially considering the fact that she knew there could be a sleeping baby inside.

"Up here!" Piper yelled back. She could tell by the giggling sounds over the baby monitor that Wyatt wasn't asleep. She wasn't surprised—it was still too early for his nap. She envied her son at the moment. It seemed like he was the only one having any fun.

"What happened to the first floor?" Phoebe asked. "It didn't look that bad when I left this morning. Did I miss another demon?"

"Nope," Piper answered. "Just the cleaning service I hired."

"You do know they were supposed to make the place look better, not worse?" Phoebe said.

"Although they did get that disgusting green sludge off the floor."

"I think someone was trying to mess with me," Piper said, turning another page. "Pun fully intended."

Piper relayed her story of the cleaning service with the odd payment policy. Saying it out loud didn't make it sound any less insane. Luckily, judging from Phoebe's reaction, it appeared that Piper had done exactly what any normal person would have done in the situation.

"Well, this isn't good," Phoebe said. "What did this Mr. Goode look like?"

"Tall . . . dark . . . handsome," Piper said. "You know, the typical demon we get around here."

"Not a blonde?" Phoebe asked.

"Nope," Piper said. "His hair was darker than mine . . . or even yours, this week. Why do you ask?"

"You're not the only one who had a strange visitor this morning," Phoebe said. She then relayed a similar story, about an IT guy who had behaved rather strangely at work. Though the descriptions of the two men were different, there were definite similarities between the stories. The most notable was that each man seemed to think he was entirely in the right about what he had done.

"Do you think these guys are part of a team of demons?" Phoebe asked.

"Maybe," Piper said. "But I can't figure out their motivation."

"Well, in the long list of demons we've encountered, these don't seem too threatening," Phoebe said.

"No, but they're certainly annoying," Piper said as she continued to flip through the Book. She figured there was even less of a chance she would find information on a gang of Computer Support/Cleaning Demons, but she wasn't ready to give up yet.

"Oh, I almost forgot," Phoebe said as she pulled a business card out of her purse. "When I touched the guy's card, I heard something like a trumpet."

"Did you see anything?"

"No," Phoebe replied. "Only sound. No video."

"Maybe the demons play in a jazz band," Piper suggested sarcastically as she turned another page in the Book.

"I still can't figure out why I only heard a noise but didn't see anything," Phoebe said.

"Just add it to the list of questions," Piper said.

Phoebe picked up the Yellow Pages that Piper had brought up to the attic with her. It was opened to the full-page ad that had caught Piper's attention only hours earlier.

Piper had known that she should have been more suspicious of a cleaning service that could show up at a moment's notice, but at the time it had just seemed like a stroke of luck. *Yeah*, Piper thought, looking back. *Bad luck.*

"Is this the guy?" Phoebe asked. "Goode's Cleaning Service?"

"That's him," Piper said. "What was your guy's name?"

"Robert Fellows," Phoebe said, reading the name off the business card. "Hey, wait. I think I found something." She put the card down under the ad and held it up for her sister to see.

Piper looked down at the now familiar ad. Phoebe had folded the business card in half and placed it over the name of the cleaning service. Now the two names stood beside each other, making one name.

"Goodfellows?" Piper read. "The mob's after us?"

"Is there such a thing as a demon mob?" Phoebe wondered aloud.

"If there is, it would be only natural that they found us," Piper said.

Although they were joking around, the two sisters looked at each other with dread.

As they tried to figure out if the names were linked, the third Charmed One orbed into the attic, clearly in a huff.

"I need that," Paige said as she pushed her way past her sisters to where the Book of Shadows sat on a table.

"Don't worry," Phoebe said as she grabbed Paige by the arm. "We're already on it."

"Already on what?" Paige asked.

"Let me guess," Piper said. "You ran into a

seemingly well-intentioned stranger who pulled a prank on you. Something destructive, but not quite harmful?"

Paige looked at Piper, surprised but still steamed. "So, I'm not the only one this happened to?"

"Nope, I'm afraid not. Where's your gear, by the way?" Phoebe asked, growing more suspicious by the moment.

"Down the river," Paige replied.

"Well, since we've already dealt with a blonde and a brunette, I'm guessing you got the redhead," Piper said.

"Auburn hair, actually," Paige corrected. "And twinkling green eyes."

"Oh, yeah," Piper said. "The eyes. My guy's were blue."

"Gray," Phoebe said.

"So we're dealing with three guys with twinkling eyes?" Paige asked as she watched Piper continue flipping through the Book of Shadows. "Sounds like a bad fifties group. Somehow I doubt they'd be in there under that name."

"Did your guy give you a card, by any chance?" Phoebe asked.

"No," Paige said. "Just a flower. But he told me his name was Robin, if that helps."

"Robin?" Phoebe asked as she took the Book of Shadows from Piper. "As in Robin Goodfellow."

Paige's eyes went wide. "You don't mean—"

"I *knew* that quote was familiar," Phoebe interrupted. "The IT guy changed my column to read 'Gentles, do not reprehend. If you pardon, I will mend.' It was from *A Midsummer Night's Dream*. We're not being stalked by a demon mob. If I'm not mistaken, we're all being bothered by the same guy. And even though we've never met him, I think we all know his name."

Even though Phoebe hadn't known what page to go to, she immediately landed on the entry she had been looking for.

Piper saw the page over her sister's shoulder and in an instant understood the identity of the demon. "Puck."

Chapter 5

"So we're dealing with a character from Shakespeare?" Paige asked. "Damn that bard. What's next, Hamlet's ghost?"

"So instead of three demons, we've got one that's a master of disguise and can move about town in the blink of an eye," Piper said, summing up their suspicions. "This just keeps getting better."

"Well, this is fairly useless," Phoebe said as she read over the passage on Puck, a.k.a. Robin Goodfellow, in the Book of Shadows. Never before had she seen a more confusing jumble of words and meaningless phrases.

"No information?" Piper asked.

"Just the opposite," Phoebe replied. "Too much information. And all of it is contradictory. Things are crossed out with arrows pointing here and there. It's a mess. As far as I can tell, the Warren witches have run into him from time to time, but no two experiences have been the same."

Phoebe skimmed over the page again. The Book of Shadows had been passed down through the maternal line of her ancestry for generations. Each woman would add what she had learned about magic and the demons she had encountered along the way.

The interesting thing about the Book was that it kept growing. And not just from the entries of the witches currently entrusted with the Book. Just because a particular witch had died didn't mean that she was through passing along her wisdom. There were many occasions in which the Charmed Ones opened up the Book and found information that had previously not been there.

The page on Puck—or Robin Goodfellow— looked like the Warrens had been adding to it constantly over the past few centuries. In fact, the entry went on for nearly three pages, even though there was probably only a page and a half of actual information between the scratched-out text and partial notes.

Piper and Paige listened as Phoebe tried to make out what she could from the hodgepodge of writings.

"According to the Book, Puck is either a fairy, a hobgoblin, an imp, a pixie"—Phoebe paused and looked at her sisters with dread—"or the devil himself."

"Well, that's new," Piper said.

"Somehow I doubt the devil would waste his

time playing practical jokes," Paige said. "I imagine he or she would be saving something bigger for us."

"Goody," Phoebe said. "Something to look forward to."

"And all the fairies we've met have been much smaller than the guy who came to the house today," Piper added. "And had wings. Although the temperament was kind of the same."

"I don't think he's any of those things," Phoebe said. "It looks like Robin, or Puck, is one of a kind."

"What's with the multiple names?" Paige asked. "Is he Puck or Robin?"

"Actually, he's both," Phoebe said. "It looks like—historically—Puck and Robin Goodfellow were two different beings, but eventually they either merged into one, or people realized they were one, or something happened where one of them disappeared and the other took his place. It's not very clear."

"It never is," Piper muttered.

"Either way, he's been around forever and he goes by a ton of different names. If this book were better cross-referenced we'd be flipping through it for hours checking out all the entries."

"Where's a good footnote when you need one?" Paige quipped.

"How bad is it?" Piper asked.

"I can't tell for sure," Phoebe said. "Some say

Puck's just a mischief-maker—which we've seen firsthand—while others . . . well, let's just say that some stories are closer to that part about him being the devil."

"Let me guess, he has a long list of different powers, too," Paige said. "Each more deadly than the next?"

"Sort of," Phoebe replied. "It looks like there's a consensus on him being a shape-shifter—which, again, we've seen for ourselves. Although some think he might be a changeling. But that could just have something to do with the fact that people often get the two confused."

"We know he has at least two different disguises," Piper said. "Though I doubt any of us saw his true face."

Phoebe continued to work her way through the mess of information. "It's unclear how powerful he really is and what he can really do."

"Well, this thing is fairly useless," Paige said, dismissing the Book with a wave of her hand as if it had intentionally left out information.

"Any idea what he wants with us?" Piper asked. "I doubt he just felt like dropping by and then continuing on his merry way."

"I hope he comes back," Paige said. "He owes me a cell phone, some camping equipment, and a new outfit. Not to mention a backpack. And this stuff isn't exactly cheap."

"Add that to the bill for the destruction of the first floor," Piper said.

"And I suspect he's going to bill Elise for the service call," Phoebe said.

"So what do we do now?" Piper asked. "Just wait for him to come back?"

"I say we go looking for him," Paige said. "Maybe scry for him with the business card. There has to be some way to—" Paige stopped mid-sentence, clutching her stomach. Her face had gone white, with tinges of blue.

"Paige? What's wrong?" Phoebe asked.

"I don't know," Paige replied, looking curiously ill. "I feel—"

Paige doubled over in pain. Before her sisters could rush to her side, she burst into hundreds of blue and white orbs. It looked like she was orbing somewhere, but the orbs never left the room. They just hovered in midair like fireflies swarming together.

"Paige!" Phoebe cried as she hurried to the orbs.

"Don't touch anything," Piper warned as Phoebe moved toward her orbing sister. "There's no telling what the orbs might do to you."

"What's going on?" Phoebe asked as she examined the floating orbs. "Have you ever seen this before? You know, before the pranks began?"

"No," Piper said. "But I think I know who's behind it."

"No kidding," Phoebe agreed. It was fairly obvious someone was toying with them. This time, the game was especially cruel.

"Ho, ho, ho."

Phoebe and Piper heard the laughter before they saw the source of it.

"Enough with the exposition," Puck said as he shimmered into the room. "Can we get to the action already?"

"Puck!" Phoebe said.

"Speak of the devil," Puck said, with a bow, "and the devil appears."

This version of Puck was slightly different from the three that had visited the Charmed Ones earlier in the day. He was tall and lean, like the others, but there was something about the way he carried himself. He seemed to be in constant motion, even though he was standing still.

Puck's long, flowing hair was pure white, which made his purple eyes even more pronounced. His ears did not end in points like the traditional image Phoebe had in her head; instead, they were slightly more rounded than the average human ear—like circles, not ovals. It was just enough to make them look different without calling too much attention to them. In his left ear he wore a row of earrings running from top to bottom. He looked to be in his midtwenties, though from what was written in the Book of Shadows, he was at least several centuries beyond that age.

His clothing was another story entirely. The subdued overalls, business-casual apparel, and hiking outfit had been replaced by a flashy blue suit with a sequined collar. He even had a red handkerchief peeking out of the breast pocket, which matched the silk shirt he was wearing underneath. He had chosen to complete the look with a black tie that looked like someone had stretched out a Slinky.

"Put Paige back together," Piper insisted.

Puck simply laughed at her. "Did you ever notice when a phrase like 'put Paige back together' became normal, everyday language for you gals?"

"What do you want from us?" Phoebe asked.

"What makes you think you have anything I would want?" Puck asked.

"Then why are you doing this?" Piper asked.

"Boredom. Slow-news day," Puck replied. "Wouldn't you say so, Phoebe? You are the resident expert nowadays, are you not?"

With a wave of his hand, he sent Paige's orbs floating around the room.

"Stop that," Phoebe said.

"No," Puck replied.

"Look," Piper said with barely contained anger, "Puck, or Robin, or whatever you call yourself—"

"I call myself many things," Puck said. "Though not as many things as others may call me."

"Well, whoever you are—" Phoebe began.

"I think that should be *whomever*," Puck said as he made Paige's orbs do a loop in the air. "Or, *is* it *whoever*? I never do get that right. Back when I started school, we didn't have English classes. We didn't have *English*, for that matter. Or maybe we did. You know, my history is so confusing, even I sometimes forget where I came from."

"Puck!" Piper and Phoebe said simultaneously, trying to shut him up.

"That's my name," he said. "Wait, we've established that already. And really I understand why you'd be jealous of my many names. I mean, your family doesn't show much creativity when it comes to choosing monikers, do you? Piper, Phoebe, Paige, Prue, Patty, Penelope. Please, that's positively pedestrian in a pedantic pedigree, if you ask me. And don't even get me started at the lack of originality in little Wyatt Matthews's name."

"We just want to know how to make you stop bothering us," Piper said. She was tired of him rambling on and on without making any sense.

"Touché." Puck grinned. "I like you."

"Thanks," Piper said, dryly. "That means a lot."

"Wait a minute," Puck said, his face lighting up. "*My* name begins with a 'P,' too! Hey, will you gals adopt me? I've always wanted a mom . . . or three."

"Can we vanquish this guy already?" Phoebe asked, checking the Book for a spell.

"Tsk, tsk, tsk," Puck said, waving an extraordinarily long finger at Phoebe. It was growing longer by the second.

Using that same finger, he directed Paige's orbs to spin in an arc that went up to the ceiling and down to the floor. "You don't just go around vanquishing everyone who comes across your path, do you?" he asked. "I mean, what have I done that was so wrong? Other than add some excitement to an otherwise boring day?"

"Well, for one thing, you're currently juggling our sister," Piper said through gritted teeth.

"Okay, good point," Puck said. The orbs stopped spinning, but they still didn't turn back into Paige. "Is that better?"

"Can we just cut to the chase?" Phoebe asked. "Threaten us. Try to do us harm. Anything, so we can get on with the vanquishing."

"My, but she's a violent one," Puck said. He emphasized the comment by scattering Paige's orbs throughout the room and watching as they bounced their way back together.

"Boingee, boingee, boingee," he repeated as the orbs returned to one another.

"She's not the only violent one in the room," Piper said. "We've gotten pretty good at taking care of demons that get in our way."

"Demon!" Puck said, revealing what could have passed for genuine anger. "Where in there does it say I'm a demon?"

Puck pushed past Phoebe and went for the Book of Shadows. Phoebe noticed that the book didn't slam shut when he approached it, but he hadn't actually tried to touch it either.

"I don't see any mention of a demon in here," Puck said. "Nope. About a hundred other names, but no demon. Devil comes the closest, but do I look like the devil to you? . . . Don't answer that."

Puck ignored the sisters for a moment as he read down the page, mumbling as he went. He then scrunched up his face as if he had read something he didn't like. "Oh, but that's entirely wrong. You girls really need to update this. No one's gotten away with calling me a fairy since that Kipling fellow—"

He looked at Phoebe. "Do you like Kipling?"

Phoebe was about to answer, but then she realized he was setting her up for an old vaudeville routine. "I don't know. I've never kippled."

"Now, I came up with that one," Puck said regretfully. "Wish I got royalties every time that joke was used in the thirties, forties, and fifties. I'd be a rich—well, wait . . . I *am* a rich—"

"Enough with the floor show," Piper said, raising her hands threateningly. "What do you want?"

"Hands down, hands down," Puck said. "I'm not your enemy. Not yet, anyway."

That put Phoebe on edge. "What's that supposed to mean?"

"I've heard so much about you lovely ladies that I figured it was time I properly introduced myself," Puck said, holding out a hand to Phoebe. "Hi, I'm Puck, Robin, Pwca, Phouka, Pooka, Puca—et cetera—Goodfellow. Pleased to meet you."

Phoebe refused to take his hand.

"Well, if you're going to be that way," Puck said, pulling his hand back. "Anyway, I have come to determine the true nature of your being."

"Okay," Phoebe said. "What does that mean?"

"In short," Puck said, "I want to find out if you are a good witch or a bad witch."

"You have *got* to be kidding me," Piper said.

"Um, obviously you haven't done your research, Puck," Phoebe said. "We're good witches. The best, some might say."

"Really?" Puck put his hands on his hips. Paige's orbs bounced up and down like they were on a trampoline. "It's interesting that you say that. Because I've heard differently in the circles that I've traveled."

"Maybe you need to travel in better circles," Phoebe said.

"Yes, well, that's neither here"—Puck sent Paige's orbs sailing across the room—"nor there. And, quite frankly, my opinion is the only one that matters. In order to form this opinion, I have devised a little test."

"I can't wait to hear this," Piper said.

"Oh, no need to worry," Puck said. "It's nothing you need to study for. In fact, it's right up your alley. Pop quiz time!"

"We're not about to jump through any of your hoops," Phoebe said.

"What a fitting choice of phrase," Puck said as a pink and white floating hoop appeared in the air. Not surprisingly, he sent Paige's orbs through the hoop over and over again.

"As you may or may not know," Puck continued as the orbs did their act, "the circus has recently come to town."

"Obviously one of the clowns got loose," Phoebe said.

Puck belched out a laugh. "Oh, that was precious. Do you mind if I use it?"

Phoebe waved him off. She was ready for him to get to the point.

"Anyway," Puck continued, "there's a—what do you call them? An Innocent? Someone in danger, in need of your help."

Piper gave a slight nod.

"An *Innocent*," Puck said, trying out the word. "How quaint. Like anyone is truly innocent nowadays."

"Get to the point," Piper said, barely containing her exasperation.

"Yes, well, there's an Innocent at the circus in need of protection," Puck said. "Go there, do your job, save the Innocent, and then I'll decide whether you're worthy of being my friend or my enemy."

"And what if we don't want to be your friends?" Phoebe asked.

Suddenly, all humor went out of Puck's face and a noticeable pall fell over the room. "Trust me," he said, "you don't want to be my enemy."

Piper and Phoebe shot each other a look. Instinctively they knew that, all jokes aside, this was not a being to mess with.

"But don't worry," Puck said, suddenly jovial again. "I grade on a curve."

"And what do *we* get out of this?" Phoebe asked.

"Correct me if I'm wrong, but isn't there some kind of personal gain penalty?" Puck asked. "And really, whatever happened to the work being its own reward?"

"Oh, we'll help the Innocent if there really is one," Piper said. "She meant, why should we believe anything you tell us? You haven't exactly been straight with us so far today."

Puck let out an exaggerated sigh. "Oh, very well." He snapped his fingers. "There. The Manor is spotless. And I won't even ask for clothing in exchange."

"What about my column?" Phoebe asked.

"Well, now, I do still have some concerns about that," Puck said. "But we can discuss them later." He gave another snap of his fingers. "All better."

"And Paige's backpack," Piper said.

"Well now, that's a real problem," Puck said. "See, this momma bear fished it out of the river and gave it to her cubs. And they've been using it as a sort of litter box. So, I doubt that Paige would want it back."

Piper and Phoebe didn't know whether to believe him or not, but they both figured they had gotten just about all the generosity they were going to get out of him for now.

"Okay," Piper said. "Who is this Innocent that needs saving?"

"I guess I *could* tell you," Puck said, a grin once again plastered on his face. "But where's the fun in that?"

With that last remark, Puck's body started to fade away. First his feet disappeared, then his hands and arms. Then, slowly, the rest of him evaporated until all that was left was his smile, hanging midair like the Cheshire Cat's.

"I just love a classic exit," the disembodied mouth said before it faded out of sight. Even though he was gone, they could still hear the echo of his "Ho, ho, ho," laughter bouncing against the attic walls.

Piper and Phoebe looked at each other as if they didn't believe what they had just witnessed. Then they realized that something was still amiss.

"Hey," Piper yelled into the empty air. "Give us back our sister!"

Chapter 6

"Does someone want to tell me what just happened?" Paige asked the moment her body returned to normal. "I feel like I just got off an amusement park ride."

Piper and Phoebe quickly filled Paige in on what she had missed. They delicately avoided saying anything about Puck sending her orbs around the room like she was a laser light show. When they finished, the only sound in the attic was Wyatt's crying coming through the baby monitor.

"That horrible imp, hobgoblin, pixie-man," Paige said in disgust. "He really wouldn't return my backpack?"

"I don't think that's what our focus should be on at the moment," Piper said. Wyatt's crying was getting louder and more insistent.

"Especially if there's really an Innocent that needs our help," Phoebe added.

"Well, what are we waiting for?" Paige asked

as she moved toward the attic door. "Off to the circus."

"Wait a minute," Piper said, grabbing Paige's arm. "You're not seriously going to believe Puck, are you? This could be some kind of trap. We've all seen firsthand how much he likes to play games."

Though she had no intention of leaving the house, Piper continued to walk out of the attic and down to the nursery. She recognized Wyatt's cry was of the "change me" variety. If he stayed on schedule, he should be hitting her with the "I'm hungry" cry soon. Then, as soon as he was full, his eyes would droop and he'd want to be put down for a nap.

It was odd—and somewhat annoying—that the only part of her life that kept to a schedule was her baby. This was supposed to have been her day to get the place clean and do some of her own chores. The most irritating part of the whole situation was that it was technically her day off. Unfortunately, P3 was the only one of her jobs from which she was allowed to take time off. Though, really, she shouldn't take too much time off since she was the club's owner.

"If there's an Innocent in trouble, we have to do something," Paige said as she and Phoebe followed Piper into the nursery. "Don't we?"

"If we knew for a fact there was an Innocent involved, then yes," Phoebe said. "But we don't know that for sure. All we know is what Puck told us and, if you ask me, his credibility is a bit questionable at the moment."

"But how will we know unless we investigate?" Paige asked. "It's a classic catch-22."

"If someone we're supposed to help is in trouble, then our paths will cross somehow," Piper said as she picked up Wyatt. By scent alone she could tell she was right in identifying the cause of his tears. "That's how it usually happens. We don't often get formal invitations. Or challenges, as in this case."

Piper carried Wyatt over to the changing table.

"What if that's how it works this time?" Paige asked. "What if Puck was supposed to tell us about the Innocent?"

"She's got a point," Phoebe said.

Piper threw out the old diaper. She had thought Phoebe would have stayed on her side for at least a little longer. "What if it's his way of getting us out of the Manor so he can steal the Book of Shadows, or harm Wyatt, or tap into the Nexus? I'm just saying we need to be cautious."

"When *aren't* we cautious?" Paige asked.

"Do you really need me to run down that list?" Piper said. "We do have a tendency to rush into trouble at times."

"Okay," Phoebe said. "But I think this conversation alone proves that this isn't one of those times."

Piper considered what her sisters were saying.

She knew they were right, but that didn't make it any easier to accept what she had to do. "I don't like this," she said.

"Neither do I," Paige admitted. "But we can't just ignore an Innocent because we don't like the messenger."

"I *really* don't like the messenger," Piper said. Just because Puck supposedly fixed the mess he had made down on the first floor, it didn't make up for what he had put them through that morning.

Piper once again thought of all the errands and chores around the house she was supposed to be doing. She had been looking forward to crossing things off her to-do list. Puck had taken up enough of her time. But, she knew that if an Innocent was at stake, that trumped cleaning out the refrigerator.

"Me neither," Paige insisted. "But that shouldn't stop us from calling Leo to come down here to watch Wyatt so we can get to the circus."

"Actually, we can't call Leo," Piper said. "He's at a Whitelighters and Elders retreat. He'll be out of touch all day."

"You're kidding," Phoebe said. "You mean they all leave their charges unattended for an entire day?"

"Wait a minute," Paige said. "They actually have a *retreat*? What do they have to retreat from? Don't the Elders just sit around all day watching life pass them by and give out vague, usually unhelpful, information?"

"Don't ask me," Piper said as she finished changing her son. "Apparently it's one of the perks of the job."

"That, and a good dental plan," Phoebe joked.

"Can't you call a sitter?" Paige asked.

"On such short notice? I don't think so. It's not like we can just leave Wyatt with anyone, you know," Piper replied.

"What if we need the Power of Three?" Paige asked.

Piper picked Wyatt up and held him to her chest. He had stopped crying and was now softly cooing. "Let's not move so fast," she said. "You two go and scope out the situation. Come back here when you're done. In the meantime, I'll go online and see if I can find any more concrete information on Puck."

"Is Puck really our main concern at the moment?" Paige asked.

"Yes," her sisters replied at the same time.

"Just asking," Paige said.

"For the record, I'm not crazy about us splitting up like this," Phoebe said. "Since we don't know what to expect."

"I don't like it either," Piper admitted. "But this is one circus I'm not about to bring Wyatt to."

Chapter 7

"What did we ever do before orbing?" Phoebe asked the moment after she and Paige had transported into the circus grounds without having to pay for tickets at the main gate.

"If only we could use it for concerts and shows," Paige agreed. "Imagine the money we'd save."

"If you ask me, I think we'd find plenty of Innocents at a rock concert," Phoebe said. "We could probably find a way around that personal gain clause if we really tried."

"Maybe we should look into it," Paige suggested. "It would be sort of like writing things off on your taxes. As long as we can justify the use of magic—"

"I was kidding," Phoebe said.

"So was I," Paige added quickly.

But there was something in Paige's tone that made Phoebe suspect her sister would have tried to get away with it if she could. Phoebe just chalked it up to the fact that Paige was still a relative newbie when it came to her magical gifts. She had never been sent to the future to see just how dangerous abusing the personal gain clause could be.

Aside from saving them a few bucks on admission, Paige's orb had managed to get them onto the grounds much faster than if they had been forced to wait in line. Therefore, they weren't violating the clause.

The circus fairgrounds were packed with people. Phoebe was amazed by the number of adults who were off from work in the middle of the day. Then again, she was technically off, as well. At least from her day job.

There was a childlike excitement in the air that Phoebe suspected was more a product of her own imagination than any real energy. Then again, she had experienced many strange things since learning she was a witch. It was entirely possible that childhood excitement could be transferred into some kind of tangible energy.

She found that thought sobering. It had just hit her that with all these children around, Puck's warning that an Innocent was in trouble held a much greater meaning. Sure, they were dealing with a prankster, so it was hard to take things too seriously. But if the children were in danger, Phoebe knew that the time for joking was over.

"I don't know," Paige said as she looked out

over the fairgrounds. "The circus isn't quite the way I remembered it. Where's the sawdust? The big top? The tattooed lady?" She looked directly at Phoebe, who sported some herself. "Cancel that last one."

Phoebe gave her sister a playful slap. *Okay, maybe a few lighthearted jokes will ease the tension*, she thought.

She had to agree with Paige: The circus seemed very different from how it had been when she was a child. Grams had taken her, Piper, and Prue once, many years ago. It certainly hadn't been a world-renowned circus like the Fletcher Family Circus they were currently attending. It had been a much smaller affair, and far more like the kind of circus that was portrayed in books and movies. Phoebe had been awfully young at the time, but she remembered that there had been grassy fairgrounds, an honest-to-goodness big top, and even a very un-PC freak show that still gave her chills. And that was saying something, considering the freaks she now dealt with on an almost daily basis.

The Fletcher Family Circus had none of that. First of all, the big top had been replaced by the concrete Cow Palace. The Palace, as it was known informally, was an indoor arena on the border of San Francisco and Daly City. It could accommodate thousands more people than even the largest tent could hold, but in its vastness it definitely lost something in the aesthetic appeal of the big top. Traditionally, the place hosted concerts, sporting events, and various activities brought in by groups renting out the space.

The fairgrounds essentially consisted of a sectioned-off area of a large parking lot where the atmosphere was most like a carnival, with animals on display, street performers, cotton candy machines, and music playing in the background.

There was no freak show like the one Phoebe had seen as a child, but in the current age, that wasn't much of a surprise. Considering that the tightrope walkers had been replaced by "Wire Walkers," and the trapeze artists were now known as "Sky Surfers," the lack of freaks was perfectly understandable.

That didn't mean that there weren't freaks around—this was the San Francisco area, after all—but none of them were sanctioned by the Fletcher Family Circus.

A quick search online had informed Phoebe that the circus gates opened two hours before the matinee started so the public could walk "amongst the animals" on the asphalt fairgrounds. The Charmed Ones had decided that this would be the best way to mingle among the circus workers and see what they could discover.

"Where should we start?" Paige asked as she surveyed the grounds.

It was a fairly chaotic scene. The place was packed. Children were pulling their parents around to look at animals in pens and cages. The attractions ranged from dogs to llamas to lions. Circus employees were scattered about, giving demonstrations of what was to come once the show started, and clowns were playing with the children and making their parents look like fools. It was a child's wonderland, which could all go horribly wrong with one evil demon added into the mix.

Although the crowds made it easier for Phoebe and Paige to snoop around unnoticed, there was a lot of ground to cover and a lot of potential Innocents to consider.

"Somehow, I doubt if we just stand here our Innocent will approach us," Phoebe said.

As if to openly mock what she had said, a large clown stumbled up to Phoebe a second later, purposely knocking into her in an exaggerated—but still painful—gesture as his oversize red plastic shoe stepped on her clogs. To make matters worse, she could tell that he was scuffing the leather.

"Although stranger things have happened," Phoebe said.

"You can say that again," Paige said.

The clown gave Phoebe a sad look as if he felt horribly about bumping into her. He lifted his tiny blue bowler hat, which also raised his red wig off his head. Beneath the wig was a bald head that had been painted with red and white concentric circles that made his scalp look like a

bull's-eye. He had obviously intended the art-
work to be seen, or else he would never have
applied the makeup job in the first place.

The kids around them all stopped in their
tracks. They were smart enough to know that
there was about to be a show and they were
already cracking up over the foolish clown with
his target-covered bald head.

"Okay, thanks," Phoebe said as she tried to
extricate herself from the performance. She
immediately had a flashback of a semi-repressed
scene from the circus she had attended with
Grams, in which a clown had pretended to sit in
her lap and had accidentally crushed her cotton
candy in the process. Granted, in the great
scheme of things, there were much more horrific
memories to repress, but it had been scary to her
at the time.

The clown she was presently with grabbed
her by the arm and pulled her back into his act.

"Really, it's okay," she said, trying to walk
away again. "No harm. No foul."

The clown waved his hands in front of her
like he needed to make amends for bumping
into her. Phoebe wanted to tell him that just
leaving her alone would be apology enough, but
it was very hard to be rude to a clown when she
was standing in an ever-growing circle of children. She could already imagine herself making
the clown cry and then getting booed by all the
children.

The clown seemed to feel like a gift would be appropriate penance for his misstep. He reached inside his bright yellow jacket, looking for something to give Phoebe, and triumphantly pulled out a rubber chicken.

"Didn't see that one coming," Paige joked.

Phoebe shot her sister a "help me" look.

"Sorry," Paige said. "You're on your own with this one."

The clown shook his head and stuffed the chicken back in his jacket. He continued searching, making sure to turn around so that all of the children could see what he was doing. This time, he pulled a pair of boxer shorts from his jacket.

This sent the children into hysterics. Apparently jokes about underwear were classic, as far as kids were concerned. Phoebe just felt embarrassed for the grown man.

The clown hastily shoved the underwear back into his jacket. Phoebe hoped that the routine would be over soon. She knew from a writing class she had taken in college that comedy usually occurred in threes. Therefore, whatever he pulled out of his jacket next would finish the act and then she could get on with finding her Innocent. Unless, of course, this was the Innocent that she had been looking for.

As I said, to Paige, she thought regretfully, *stranger things have happened.*

This time, the clown pulled something smaller out of his jacket, but he kept it covered in his hands so that no one could see it. He made a big deal of acting shy and embarrassed about giving it to her. He was so convincing that even Phoebe was beginning to wonder what it was.

After an extended back-and-forth in which the clown seemed to debate whether to give the item to Phoebe, he finally dropped to one knee and held it up for everyone to see. It was a purple ring with a huge plastic "diamond" approximately the size of a golf ball. She had seen gaudier jewelry in her time, but no one had ever presented her with such a bauble.

"Oh, no," Phoebe said, deciding that the only way to get the act over with was by playing along with it. "I simply couldn't. It's way too soon. We've just met."

"Go ahead," Paige said. "I'd gladly approve of *this* marriage."

Phoebe glared at her sister. "Well, okay," she said, making sure all the children could hear her. "I accept."

The clown slipped the ring onto her finger and then jumped up several feet into the air. Phoebe thought he must have had some kind of spring device in his shoes because it seemed nearly impossible for a human being to bounce that high on his own.

Eventually, the clown settled down, firmly planted on his oversize feet. Before she could walk away, he pulled Phoebe into a huge hug, and she suddenly found herself wrapped up in his baggy, colorful costume. The clown had an unusually strong grip on her, and she was afraid she was going to be smothered.

Once Phoebe extricated herself from the clown, he waved "good-bye" to her and hurried off to his next victim.

"That is so indicative of my love life," Phoebe lamented. "Just when I get a guy, he goes running off."

"At least you got to keep the ring," Paige said.

"Yeah," Phoebe said as she slipped it off her finger and—making sure the children weren't watching—deposited it in the nearest trash can.

"What did you do that for?" Paige asked.

"I learned long ago that it's not safe to accept gifts from strangers," Phoebe said. "Especially ones with painted faces."

"Good point," Paige said. "So, now that we've gotten past the comedic portion of our program, what's the plan?"

"Beats me," Phoebe said as she took in their surroundings. It was impossible to think that they were going to stumble across their Innocent in the mass of people around them.

There has to be a more logical way to do this, Phoebe thought. As she continued to scan the fairgrounds, she tried to pick up on the vibes of the people around her. She opened her mind, searching for some kind of sign indicating what she should do, but nothing came. She thought about randomly picking up things around her and trying to get a premonition, but that seemed about as logical as going from person to person and asking if he or she was her Innocent.

Phoebe closed her eyes for a moment, hoping that by shutting out all the stimulation around her she might be able to come up with a plan of attack. But all that she could focus on was the circus music floating through the air. It sounded like an old-fashioned brass band was playing somewhere on the fairgrounds. "That's it!" she said.

"What's it?" Paige asked. "What did I miss?"

"My premonition," Phoebe said. "From when I touched Puck's business card."

"The trumpet sound?" Paige asked.

"Exactly," Phoebe said. "We need to find the bandstand."

Phoebe took off in the direction of the music.

"Don't you think you're being a little literal?" Paige asked as she followed her sister.

"It's all we have to work off of," Phoebe said as she weaved her way through the crowd. She had to stop herself before tripping over a few crying children who failed to move out of her way. The kids managed to get underfoot with surprising speed. Phoebe figured it had to have something to do with their inability to see through eyes filled with tears. *They're probably scared of the clowns*, she thought. *I don't blame them.*

The music was getting louder, but it was hard to peer through the crowd of adults gathered around the bandstand with their children. Phoebe wasn't exactly a giant, and all the fathers who were carrying their children up on their shoulders made it especially tough for her to see. Still, she kept following the music, past the games of chance, the funnel cake stand, and a man selling balloons.

"We're almost there," Phoebe said as the music grew louder. "I know our Innocent is near the source of the music. I can feel it."

The sisters passed a line of burly guys who were waiting to try their luck at a test-your-strength machine. Once Phoebe and Paige got past them, they finally saw the bandstand. It only took one look to know that they were on the wrong track entirely.

"Well, that was unexpected," Paige said.

Phoebe didn't even need to make out the identity of the trumpet player from the rest of the band members to know that her premonition had led her astray. They would not find their Innocent on the bandstand.

The band members weren't even alive. They were animatronic.

Chapter 8

"So much for my premonition," Phoebe said as she watched the mechanical band play its cheery tune. She kept an eye out for a maintenance man or anyone who may have been associated with the "band" that could be the Innocent in question. "You think Puck was playing a trick on me again? Maybe the trumpet sound has nothing to do with this."

"It's possible," Paige said. "But I don't know why he would lead us on a wild-trumpet chase."

"I don't know why he would do anything he's done so far," Phoebe said. "If you were going to ask for someone's help, would you pull a prank on them first?"

"If I thought they'd be a good sport about it," Paige said meekly.

"I really thought you'd be more bothered by this," Phoebe said.

"I'm saving my anger for the ensuing battle," Paige said. "You can tell this is going to end badly."

Phoebe nodded in agreement. She didn't need a premonition to tell her that much.

Once again she looked out over the crowded fairgrounds. More and more people were filing in as the clock ticked closer to showtime. Pretty soon, there would be thousands of people to search through.

For a brief moment, Phoebe worried that maybe *everyone* was in need of protection. But she doubted that Puck would sit by and let all these people get hurt when he could simply tell them what needed to be done. He was mischievous, but not malicious.

Wasn't he?

"Check that out," Paige said, pointing toward the fences along the edge of the fairgrounds. "What is it?"

"It looks like some kind of . . . press conference is taking place," Phoebe said.

"I've always known some politicians were clowns," Paige said, "but this is too much."

"I doubt it's political," Phoebe said.

She couldn't make out exactly what was going on, from her vantage point, but she could see some news vans parked along the edge of the gate. Conveniently, the crowds parted for a moment, and Phoebe caught a glimpse of several cameramen with their cameras all pointed at a tall, African-American man in the center of the semicircle of reporters.

"I think it's worth checking out," Paige said

as she and Phoebe started walking toward the news crews.

Phoebe wondered if anyone from her paper was there who could fill her in on what was going on. A press conference didn't seem like much of an otherworldly occurrence, but it was worth looking into. So far, it was the only thing they had seen that appeared even remotely out of place.

Phoebe couldn't imagine why anyone would be holding a press conference at the rear exit to the fairgrounds. There wasn't much going on back there. All the action was happening on the opposite side of the parking lot, where the animals and performers were entertaining the crowd. Even with her limited news experience, Phoebe knew that the circus performers made for much more interesting videotape than some guy in a suit. But when she looked past the press conference, she saw that not all the action was taking place on the fairgrounds.

Local police were holding back a small group of protesters about a hundred feet from the press conference. They didn't look particularly threatening. From where she was standing, Phoebe couldn't read their signs, but there were only a few issues that a group would be protesting outside a circus, and Phoebe could guess what this was all about. "Animal rights activists?" she wondered aloud.

"Good guess," Paige said. "Maybe Puck

wants us to take up their charge? Support animal rights?"

Phoebe looked down at her leather clogs. "Somehow I don't think he'd need the Charmed Ones for that."

Phoebe looked from her shoes to the animals in pens and cages around her. She had dated a vegetarian once, but she couldn't totally bring herself around to the cause. Still, she always treated animals well, she never wore fur, and she tried to keep real leather to a minimum in her wardrobe. Even so, she doubted that Puck had entered their lives just to give them a cause to pursue. They gave back to the community on a fairly regular basis, as far as Phoebe was concerned.

Still, she couldn't help but wonder about the health and well-being of the animals. It didn't take extensive study in zoology to realize that wearing funny outfits and performing for humans wasn't in their nature.

They look happy enough, Phoebe thought as she passed a pair of orangutans performing for the crowd. *But what do I know about animal psychology?*

She wondered if the protesters might know something sinister about the way the circus was treating the animals. That wouldn't have been the reason the Charmed Ones had been called in, but there might be a story here that the *Bay Mirror* would be interested in covering.

Phoebe pondered the idea that she and her sisters had been brought in to deal with protecting the rights of animals. It was worth looking into, in a roundabout way. Demons tended to do their best work by riling humans up. If a demon was behind the protest and getting people angry over perceived mistreatment, that demon could stir up a good-size mob over the cause. Phoebe was aware of a large number of members of the Underworld that would love to feed off that kind of anger and hatred.

"It doesn't seem like a supernatural problem to me," Paige said as she blotted her arms with a tissue. A passing child had gotten a little too close to her with his ice-cream cone.

"Still, a lead's a lead," Phoebe said as they neared the press conference.

Phoebe had to give the circus folks credit as she realized why the press conference was taking place at the back exit. The circus had positioned the event away from the main thoroughfare and behind several trailers—far enough away from the main entrance that it would go unnoticed by most of the circus-goers. Phoebe and Paige wouldn't have even seen it if they hadn't gone after the animatronic bandstand.

It was brilliant, really. By scheduling the press conference an hour before the show, whoever was in charge of public relations had managed to lead the protesters away from the main gates.

Plus, even getting a mention on the news about the protest would ultimately provide free press for the circus. It was sad to admit, but most of the viewers would probably ignore the story and only focus on the fact that the circus was in town.

By the time Phoebe and Paige reached the press conference, things were already well underway. The man in the suit that Phoebe had noticed earlier was fielding questions. It was difficult to hear anything over the noise of the protesters. It was a small bunch, but they were armed with powerful lungs.

Phoebe managed to push her way closer to the reporters. She lost Paige in the small crowd, but figured they would meet up once the group cleared out.

"I repeat," the man at the center of the press conference was saying, "there is no evidence to link the deaths of Zeus and Sabra. I assure you. . . ."

The protesters didn't seem to like that statement, because they all started jeering from their position outside the back gate. The police and circus security were keeping them tightly penned in, but it didn't look like they were a particularly rowdy group. Mainly, they were just loud, which caused Phoebe to miss what the man in the suit had just said.

It didn't matter, really, since she was still focused on the word "deaths." That was never a good sign in her line of work. Although death was fairly commonplace in the world and happened every day, Phoebe found it too much of a coincidence that this particular circus had recently experienced two deaths that may or may not have been linked. She knew that just because there was no "evidence" linking the two deaths didn't mean they weren't related—demons didn't usually leave clues that traditional human investigators would find.

Phoebe looked at each of the protesters. It was possible that one of them could be their Innocent. Actually, it was possible that any one of the thousands of people around her could be their Innocent. But Phoebe was working on instinct that she hoped came with her power of premonition. And her instincts told her that Puck had sent them there because of the two deaths. The problem was that it was hard to tell if Zeus and Sabra were humans or animals just by their names—people in the circus sometimes used exotic pseudonyms.

"Thank you," the man said in a tone that indicated he was wrapping up. "If you have any more questions, I can be reached at the number on the press release. Until then, please feel free to enjoy the circus this afternoon, on us."

One of his flunkies started moving through the crowd of reporters trying to hand out tickets. Even though Phoebe knew many reporters who would jump at the offer of freebies, none of the news people around her seemed to be chomping at the bit to attend the circus. They were already heading back to their news vans to pursue the next story.

A couple of reporters pulled aside some of the protestors for a quick sound bite. Phoebe knew that protestors usually made for good video—they were generally quite impassioned about their causes. She considered hurrying over to eavesdrop on those interviews, but then decided she'd have a better chance of getting information from a different source.

As the crowd dispersed, Phoebe saw Paige over by the fence waiting for her. Phoebe flashed her sister a smile and a quick wave to indicate she was onto something, then turned her attention to the man she hoped could give her some answers.

"Excuse me," she said, getting the PR guy's attention. "Phoebe Halliwell. *Bay Mirror.*" She quickly flashed him her press credentials without bothering to mention that she was an advice columnist and not a reporter.

"Reed Huntington," the man said in return, holding out a hand. "I was under the impression that your paper wasn't interested in covering this story. I didn't think they were sending anyone."

"Oh, you know," Phoebe said, waving off his comment, "miscommunication. I assure you, the *Mirror* is very interested in hearing the circus's side of the story."

"That's nice to hear," Reed said. "Most news agencies I've dealt with are more interested in sensationalizing the issue rather than giving it a thorough examination."

"That's the difference between TV and newspapers these days," Phoebe said.

"Really," Reed said teasingly. "I hadn't noticed there was much of a distinction between the two. Not since they started printing the newspapers in color, complete with pretty graphs and recipes for the perfect meal for a family of four."

"I assure you, the *Bay Mirror* still stands for quality reporting," Phoebe said, feeling the need to defend her coworkers. She would have felt a bit more confident if she didn't write a column that was titled "Ask Phoebe."

"That is pleasant news, indeed," he replied. Even though his words were condescending, his tone was light. Phoebe thought the man might be flirting with her.

"Do you think the circus would stand up to an in-depth report on how it treated its animals?" Phoebe asked, putting him on the defensive and betting that animal rights was indeed the cause of the press conference.

"If it couldn't, I wouldn't be working here," Reed said simply.

"So how 'bout it?" Phoebe asked.

"How 'bout what?"

"An in-depth interview?"

"How in-depth?" Reed asked, allowing Phoebe to be certain that he was flirting with her.

"As deep as I need to go," Phoebe said before she realized that the conversation was crossing some kind of professional boundary.

Apparently Reed had the same realization, because his body stiffened as he considered the request. "I think I've already stated the circus's position quite clearly."

"For a fifteen-second sound bite on the evening news," Phoebe said, slipping back into the role of the dogged reporter. "It might not even make it on the eleven o'clock report if there's some kind of food-eating contest or a sappy human interest story. I'm offering a real chance to get into the issue, to talk about what's really going on with the animals."

"I just told the press," Reed said. "We've had a couple of sick animals. There's no story. I wouldn't have called the press conference at all if the protesters hadn't forced my hand."

"There could be a story," Phoebe said, making a false threat. "The protesters could make it into one. The question is, would you rather me interview you or interview them?"

"I would hope a good journalist would be interested in both sides of the story," Reed said.

"That's why I'm talking to you first," Phoebe said. "But I guarantee that those protestors will have more to say than you say in your simple press release. And they'll say it with the kind of passion that—between you and me—my editor just loves to milk."

Reed seemed to reconsider her offer. "Okay," he finally said. "I'll give you a short one-on-one. But I hope you're prepared to hear me out."

"Naturally," Phoebe said.

"Can you meet me in the press trailer in fifteen minutes?" Reed asked. "I have some things to take care of before I can speak with you."

"Certainly," Phoebe said.

Reed gave her directions to the press trailer and handed her a pass that would let her into the restricted area, which was located on the other side of the fairgrounds, tucked among the other offices and the employees' living quarters.

"See you in fifteen minutes," she said as he turned to walk away.

"Looking forward to it," he replied.

Phoebe went to rejoin her sister. She had no idea what she was going to ask Reed, or why it was so important for her to interview him in the first place. But Phoebe had learned to trust her instincts long before she had learned she had any magical powers. For some reason, she felt that this guy was going to be able to give her some answers. She just hoped she could come up with the right questions. And that last part was entirely up to her to figure out.

"What's up?" Paige asked as Phoebe approached. "I couldn't get through the push of reporters. Why is it called a 'push,' anyway?"

"You should have felt what it was like in the middle of them," Phoebe said, by way of explanation. She then filled her sister in on what little she had learned.

"Do you need any help with your interview?" Paige asked.

"No," Phoebe replied. "But that doesn't mean you can't go with me into the restricted area and do some investigating on your own. . . ."

Chapter 9

"That's okay, honey," Piper said in her best soothing maternal voice. "Mommy's almost done looking up information on the weird, scary man from this morning."

Wyatt stopped fussing and gurgled something in response as if he grasped what she was saying. Piper momentarily wondered if he *had* understood her. That little boy was full of surprises. Unfortunately some of them were of the more nerve-wracking variety.

Piper put her laptop aside for a moment. She needed to take a break from the poorly designed Web sites that were based on little more than guesswork and supposition. She was even more frustrated than she had been when she'd started the research, if that was possible.

After an hour of searching online for information on Puck, she was only able to come up with details that—at best—were more confusing than what the Book of Shadows had given her.

Ignoring the sites dedicated to the wide range of literary characters that derived from Puck— ranging from *A Midsummer Night's Dream*, to various comic books, and even a Disney animated series—she tried to focus on actual mythology. Still, nothing paid off.

On the other hand, she had learned a few things of interest. First and foremost was the fact that Puck's proposition to exchange clothing for cleaning services was one of the most ancient facets of his mythology. That aspect of Puck's character was even the inspiration for a certain little character in a widely known book/movie series about a different breed of witches and wizards.

At least now she didn't feel like such a fool for falling for his trickery. Although the knowledge that she wasn't the first in history to be *Pouk-ledden* didn't make her feel any better about trusting that there was an Innocent in need of help from the Charmed Ones.

"Here we go, Wyatt," Piper said as she lifted her son from his playpen and bounced him in her arms. His giggles indicated that this was one of his favorite activities.

Piper had taken her son into the conservatory so she could be near him while she did her research. Between her job at P3 and the constant demon interference, she felt like she was always missing out on the important moments in Wyatt's life. She had already missed the first time he rolled over on his own, and she dreaded the day someone else told her that he was walking.

"So, what do you think about this Puck fellow?" she asked Wyatt. "You're not sensing anything, are you?"

Again, he gurgled in response.

"He seems harmless enough, I guess," Piper said as she looked around the conservatory. "And he did clean up his mess. That's better than some people in this house can do. And yes, I'm talking about your aunt Phoebe."

Wyatt let loose with a burst of laughter, causing Piper to stop for a moment and wonder, for the millionth time, if he really did understand her. But when he burped at the end of the laugh, she realized that he was just experiencing some well-timed gas.

"Now if we could only figure out what he's up to," Piper said. Talking out loud like this sometimes helped her work through her problems. She had been doing it for years, but she felt better now that she had a baby to talk to—she didn't feel as silly talking to herself as she had when no one was around.

After spending an hour doing research, Puck was still a mystery to her. A few sites had provided some information beyond his penchant for cleaning and clothing, and it seemed that most people seemed to agree that Puck was a hobgoblin who did not appreciate it when people mistook him for a fairy. To Piper, that seemed like a rather uninformed mistake to make. Fairies and Puck had very few similarities as far as she could tell. Certainly the size difference alone should have been enough to set people straight.

Then again, she thought, *how many average humans actually run into either fairies or Puck?*

Her Web search had also informed her that Puck liked it when people believed he was real. That actually explained more about his ego than anything else. The problem was, she doubted he'd take any pleasure in the fact that the Charmed Ones believed in him since they weren't particularly skeptics when it came to the existence of mythical beings.

Still, none of her conclusions would help them deal with Puck at the moment or give them any indication of whether he was really on their side.

"Find anything interesting?" a voice asked from behind her. "Oh, that doesn't look like me at all."

Piper spun around to find Puck leaning over her shoulder, looking at the computer screen. She had left open a site that had a painting of Puck, which looked a lot like most of the images she had seen of Pan from Greek mythology. From the look on his face, he didn't seem to like the artist's interpretation.

"I'm not that fat," he said of the picture. "Do I look that fat to you? I mean, really." He turned away from her and looked back over his shoulder.

"My butt's not that big, is it? You can tell me the truth. I'm not sensitive about my weight."

Piper considered saying a few things about him that had nothing to do with his appearance, but she figured insults would be pointless. He probably wouldn't even hear them. "What do you want?" she asked, holding Wyatt tightly.

"I thought I made that clear earlier," Puck said. "I want you to go to the circus. You shouldn't be wasting time researching me," he said as he sat down in an empty chair and crossed his legs. "I'll tell you anything you want to know."

"Somehow I doubt that," Piper said.

"Well, I didn't say I'd tell you the *truth*," Puck said. "But right now you have more important things to attend to. I could transport you to the circus, if you want. All it would take is a snap of my fingers."

"Phoebe and Paige are there right now," Piper said. "If they need me, they'll call."

"Of course they need you," Puck said. "Aren't you their leader? The calm, rational— and fairly sarcastic—one?"

"In case you haven't noticed, I have a baby here," Piper said.

"And what a cute baby he is," Puck said. "Your point?"

"My point is that I can't just leave him alone," Piper said. She couldn't believe she had to explain that to someone. "And I'm not taking

him to the circus with me, so don't even bother
suggesting it."

"That's what's wrong with society today,"
Puck said. "Overprotective mothers. How are
children ever going to learn to fend for themselves? Isn't he old enough to be left home alone
for a few hours?"

"He's not even one," Piper said.

"Exactly!" Puck said. "Why, when I was one, I
was out in the field, picking coffee beans right
next to my mother, who had given birth to me in
that very same field. Haven't you ever heard
that story?"

"Do you take credit for every joke or story
that's ever been told?" Piper asked.

"Only the fun ones," Puck said. "I let Oberon
take credit for the clunkers . . . and reality television—I had nothing to do with reality television.
Those stories are just too ludicrous to be believed."

"You know, you're a real laugh a minute."

"Hi honey, I'm home!" Leo called from the
living room. "Where are you?"

"I'm in the conservatory!" Piper yelled back.
She hadn't expected to see Leo for several hours,
but she certainly didn't mind the surprise.
"There's someone here I'd love for you to meet."

"Maybe some other time," Puck said as he
disappeared.

"Hey," Leo said as he entered the room and
kissed his wife on the cheek. "Did you say something about a guest?"

"He just left," Piper said, glancing at the clock on the wall. "You're back early."

"We're on a break, so I orbed home," Leo said as he took Wyatt from his mother's arms. "I couldn't stand being away from my two favorite people for so long."

Leo began making funny faces at Wyatt. As usual, the baby loved the performance and he laughed wildly in response.

"And you were probably getting bored Up There in the bright white land where the Elders live," Piper added. "Right?"

"Not at all," Leo said. "Our retreat is in Vegas."

"Wait a minute, you're spending the day in Vegas while I'm stuck in the house dealing with rogue cleaning crews led by crazy ancient beings?" Piper asked indignantly. "You've got to be kidding me."

"Actually, I was," Leo said, still entertaining his son with funny faces. "We're up in Elderland, like always. But what do you mean, 'crazy ancient beings' and 'rogue cleaning crews'? The place looks spotless."

"Yeah, it's a funny story," Piper said, looking around the conservatory. She had to admit the house was even cleaner than it was after the first time Puck's crew came through. "Have you ever had a run-in with a fellow named Puck, or Robin Goodfellow, or whatever name he might have gone by at the time?"

Leo's facial expression was no longer funny. In fact, it was a mask of seriousness as he put Wyatt down in his playpen. "Puck has been here? Is everyone okay?"

Piper's level of concern grew tenfold, seeing her husband's reaction. He wasn't usually one to overreact. *Well, maybe on occasion,* she thought.

"We're fine, more or less," Piper said. "We only suffered some minor property damage. But Paige had to cancel her weekend getaway, and she and Phoebe are checking into something right now."

Piper proceeded to fill Leo in on the events of the morning, starting with Puck's pranks and ending with the mission he had charged the Charmed Ones with.

"What does he really want?" Leo asked. His face was still ashen.

"That's what we want to know," Piper said. "I've spent the better part of the morning trying to figure it out." She debated mentioning that it was Puck who had stopped by a minute earlier, but figured it would only worry Leo even more.

Her husband stood in silence for a moment, turning the situation over in his mind. At one point he started to speak, but ultimately changed his mind and didn't say anything.

"Come on, Leo," Piper said. "You're scaring me. What do you know that we don't?"

"Nothing more than rumor and speculation,"

Leo said. "I've never met him, personally, but I know people who have. His reputation has changed a lot since Shakespeare wrote *A Midsummer Night's Dream*."

"Yeah," Piper said. "Apparently he had something to do with that."

"It's not all for the better," Leo said.

Piper sank into one of the wicker chairs, bracing herself. "Why do I get the feeling I'm not going to like what you're about to tell me?"

"Historically, he's been nothing but a troublemaker," Leo explained as he sat beside her, "but he's grown more powerful over the years as his story has grown. It's almost as if he's been drawing more power from the story as it's told and retold. He has even been gaining new powers as different people embellish on the story. Once something becomes part of the mythos, it becomes real to Puck."

"So he's a powerful prankster," Piper said. "I still don't see why he's a threat. If the worst he's going to do is try to mess up the house . . . well . . . we've been there before. Just yesterday, in fact. Any idea what he wants with us?"

"There's no telling, really," Leo said. "Puck is neither good nor evil—or you could say he's both good and evil, depending on how you look at it. But he is dangerous and unpredictable. The Elders have been trying to contain him for centuries with no success. Actually, I've always found him a little impressive, in that regard."

"Yeah, we know how hard it is to get around the Elders," Piper said.

"Oh, you don't know the half of it," Leo said. "I've heard some pretty wild stories."

"I'm sure you have," Piper said, though she really didn't want to hear them. She didn't need anything else to worry about at the moment. It was bad enough that Paige and Phoebe were across town and hadn't checked in yet. She didn't need anything more to fuel her imagination.

"Now that he's made contact with the Charmed Ones—" Leo took a deep breath. "I can't imagine what he's planning. I suspect that you're going to need the Power of Three to deal with it."

"Great," Piper said as she reached for the phone. "Phoebe and Paige are already on alert, but they don't have any idea what they could be up against."

Since Paige's cell phone was at the bottom of a river, Piper dialed Phoebe's line. After three rings she received what, at first, seemed to be a prerecorded message.

"We're sorry," the droning nasal voice of an operator said. "But the subscriber you are calling is currently in mortal peril—or just suffering a bad-hair day. Either way, she can't come to the phone right now. Feel free to wait for the beep to leave a message. You should hear it in about an hour. Until then, please enjoy this fine selection of Muzak, beginning with that old classic—"

Piper severed the connection before the tune could start. She really didn't care to hear Puck's musical selection.

This is not good, she thought.

"I need to get to the circus," Piper said.

"Go," Leo said. "I'll keep an eye on Wyatt."

"The Elders aren't going to like you bailing on their retreat," Piper said. She didn't really care what the Elders thought, but figured she should at least mention it so Leo knew she appreciated the trouble he was about to get into. The Elders weren't a very understanding bunch.

"They'd be more concerned if something happened to the Charmed Ones," Leo said. "You should get going. Do you want me to orb you there?"

"No," Piper said as she grabbed her car keys from the mobile that hung above the playpen. She and Wyatt had been playing with them earlier. "Until we know what Puck is up to, I want to make sure one of us is keeping an eye on Wyatt at all times."

"Okay," Leo said.

"He needs to go down for his nap, by the way," Piper said.

"Will do," Leo replied. "Now go vanquish your demon and don't worry about us."

"Hopefully I won't be gone long," Piper said, giving Leo a kiss on the cheek. Then she leaned into the playpen and blew a kiss down to Wyatt. "Be good for Daddy."

Once again, the baby gurgled in response.

Leo watched as Piper left the Manor. "There goes Mommy," he said to Wyatt. "Off to thwart evil and rid the world of demon-kind. And maybe have a little fun along the way . . . Ho, ho, ho."

Wyatt watched as his father's hair went white and grew down to his shoulders, his eyes flashed from green to purple, and his mundane, Elder-approved outfit turned into Puck's far flashier garb.

"There, that's better," Puck said. "I much prefer this look. Although throwing voices was really fun." He looked down at Wyatt in his playpen. "But you probably have no idea what I'm talking about."

Wyatt simply gurgled at him.

"That's cute, kid," Puck said. "But now, it's off to have some real fun!"

With a wave and a flourish, Puck vanished in a puff of smoke.

Baby Wyatt blinked in surprise as the smoke cleared and he saw the strange man was gone. But in the moment before he realized that he had been entirely left alone, Puck reappeared.

"Oops, silly me," Puck said to the baby. "I can't just go leaving you unattended. Mommy wouldn't like that." Puck looked around the conservatory, but didn't find anything that would be helpful.

He moved out to the hall. "I swear," he continued. "What was she thinking? Like *I'd* be going after a child. Babies aren't any fun. All they do is eat, sleep, and poop."

Puck made his way through the foyer and to the front door. He stuck his head outside and gave a little whistle. Within moments a pair of squirrels, three birds, and a raccoon came scampering and flying into the Manor.

"I need you guys to keep an eye on the baby for me," Puck told the animals as he shut the door and led them back to the conservatory. "His mother has changed him a couple times this morning, so he should be fine in that respect. He *does* need to be put down for his nap, though. And there's some milk in the fridge. If there's an emergency . . . well . . . I'm sure you'll figure something out."

And without another word—or any concern over leaving a child in the care of animals—Puck disappeared.

Chapter 10

Phoebe wound her way through the maze of circus trailers behind the Cow Palace. The pass Reed had given her had allowed her and her sister to get past security. Once they were in the off-limits area, she and Paige had split up. There was no reason for the two of them to interview Reed together. Especially considering Paige could snoop around relatively undetected as the circus performers were busy preparing for the start of the show.

After a left, a right, and another left, Phoebe found the trailer that Reed had given her directions to earlier. The sign on the door read REED HUNTINGTON, PUBLIC RELATIONS. Phoebe knocked and only waited for about a second before the door opened.

"You found me," Reed said with a look of pleasant surprise on his face. "I'm always amazed when people manage to find their way through our little circus city on their own."

"You gave very good directions," Phoebe said as she entered the small trailer and took a look around. "Nice digs."

Reed had done his best at making the crammed trailer look like a formal office. There was a desk, two guest chairs, and a file credenza, with assorted office supplies neatly arranged around the room. The fact that everything was built to a slightly smaller than average scale helped give the illusion that the space was larger than it was. It made sense that even the circus offices were built on illusion and showmanship.

As Phoebe took in her surroundings, she noticed a small blank notepad resting on the desk. She considered this a lucky break since she hadn't really come to the circus prepared to play the part of Phoebe Halliwell, Cub Reporter.

"Would you like something to drink?" Reed asked as he turned toward a small refrigerator beside the credenza. "I can offer you, well, water. Sorry, that's all I've got."

"Water will be great, thanks," Phoebe replied.

While Reed had his back to her, Phoebe picked up the notepad, along with a pen that was lying nearby, and settled into the small couch that had been hidden behind the door when Reed had welcomed her inside. She flipped over the first few pages of the notepad and scribbled a quick, nonsensical message to make it look like she was in the midst of gathering research for her story.

"I would have thought you'd have a TV in here to watch your performance on the news," Phoebe said from her perch on the surprisingly plush tiny couch.

"The televisions are in the media trailer next door," Reed said as he took two bottled waters out of the small fridge and handed one to Phoebe.

"What's back there?" Phoebe asked, pointing to a door that led to the back of the trailer.

"The bedroom," Reed said. "My office doubles as my home."

"It must cut down on your commute," Phoebe said.

"What can I say, my life is a circus," Reed said, making what Phoebe assumed was a well-practiced joke. "So you can see why I get so upset when people attack us. I wouldn't have left my comfortable home and taken on this extremely full-time job if I didn't believe the circus treated *all* of its employees with respect."

"I don't remember starting the interview," Phoebe joked lightly.

"I just want you to understand that I'm not speaking in sound bites," Reed said. "I truly believe in the work we do here."

"I'm glad to hear that," Phoebe said. "The article will come across better if you're speaking from the heart."

She did like that he was passionate about his work. It showed that he cared about more than just a paycheck. Although she did think he was pouring it on a little thick about "the work we do here." It was a circus, after all, not the headquarters of a world relief organization.

"Where would you like to begin?" Reed asked as he turned one of the guest chairs around and took a seat facing Phoebe.

"How about at the beginning," Phoebe said. "I'm sorry to say I missed the start of the press conference. And it was kind of hard to hear the Q-and-A session over the protesters."

"You'd think they'd want to hear the truth about what's happening, wouldn't you?" Reed asked. "But, no. They'd rather drown out anyone who doesn't say exactly what they want."

"Which is?"

"That the circus is releasing all the animals," Reed said.

"Is the circus releasing all the animals?" Phoebe asked.

"Not that I know of," Reed said, though there was a note of insecurity in his voice. "But nobody wants to hear that. It doesn't make for a juicy story."

"Well, now's your chance to set the record straight," Phoebe said. "With no interruptions."

Reed leaned back in his chair. He was looking at Phoebe as if he was deciding whether he could trust her. Phoebe feared she was about to lose his cooperation.

"I'll let you look over the article before I submit it to my editor," she said. It was, quite possibly, the most journalistically unethical thing she could have said. Then again, since she wasn't formally a journalist and she had no intention of writing the story, she figured she could get away with saying it with a clear conscience.

Besides, it seemed to work.

"As you know," Reed said, "it all started with Zeus."

"Of course," Phoebe lied.

"Shortly after the start of our run in Los Angeles, Zeus started dragging a little," Reed explained. "He was slow to hit his mark, and he seemed to have a general malaise about everything. I'm sure you can understand, no one wants to work with a lethargic tiger."

"Naturally," Phoebe said as she jotted "sick tiger" down on the pad to make it look like she was taking real notes. At least she was getting somewhere.

"Once his trainer consulted with the circus vet, they decided to remove Zeus from the final performances," Reed continued. "We filled his spot with Apollo."

"You have tiger understudies?" Phoebe asked.

"We have backup performers for all of the

animals and for most of the humans," Reed said. "Illnesses are just as common among animals as they are among people. Thousands of children come to see every performance. They don't want to miss out on the lions, the tigers, or the—"

"Bears?" Phoebe said.

"We don't have . . ." Reed realized that she was making a joke. "Oh . . . cute."

"Sorry." Phoebe blushed at her lame attempt at humor.

"Anyway," Reed quickly said, "parents get upset when their children are upset. Especially after paying for tickets and whatever other expenditures they may incur here."

Phoebe assumed that was a polite way of saying that an afternoon at the circus was expensive. Having orbed in for free, she wasn't about to debate that issue.

"So we have a reserve cast," Reed continued. "But that doesn't really have anything to do with the story."

"Sorry," Phoebe said again, trying to remind herself to stay on the subject. "We were talking about Zeus."

"Yes, Zeus," Reed said. There was a touch of melancholy in his tone. Phoebe wasn't surprised. She imagined if she lived and worked at the circus, she would also have a bond with the animals.

"While we were in Los Angeles," Reed continued, "his illness kept getting worse. We have

a great team of veterinarians here, but none of
the doctors had any idea what was happening.
Zeus was refusing to eat. He barely moved. It
was like he was wasting away."

"That's horrible," Phoebe said.

"It was," Reed agreed. His eyes were moist.
His concern looked genuine to Phoebe, and
she'd had a lot of practice reading people. That
particular ability was useful in both of her jobs.
"Zeus succumbed to the illness before we had
finished the run in L.A."

"I'm sorry," Phoebe said. There was a long
pause. She didn't know exactly how to phrase
her next question. "I don't mean to . . . I don't
know if . . . well, was there an autopsy?"

"Yes, actually," Reed said. "Nothing conclu-
sive was found. The vet was at a total loss to
explain Zeus's death."

Phoebe tried not to let her imagination run
wild with that last fact. There could have been a
totally reasonable explanation for the illness. But
as hard as she tried to believe it, she just couldn't
shake the suspicion that Zeus's death was not
from natural causes.

"But as they say," he continued, "the show
must go on. And so we did. We loaded up the
equipment for the trip here."

Phoebe wanted to ask more questions about
Zeus, but she figured there was only so much
that the public relations department would
know about the illness. She made a note to ask

about the vet later. He was definitely someone worth "interviewing." For now, she had to move this interview forward. "You had mentioned Zabra . . . or—"

"Sabra," Reed corrected her. "S-a-b-r-a."

Phoebe quickly wrote down the name as he spelled it.

"She was a beautiful white Lipizzaner," Reed said. "She had been with the circus longer than Zeus. As the crews were loading up the animals for the ride north to San Francisco, our horse trainer noticed that his star steed was also looking peaked. She didn't even make it through the train ride up."

"You've lost a tiger and a horse?" Phoebe asked, trying to make sense of the path the illness was spreading. "I wouldn't think they interacted much."

"They don't," Reed said. "We can't figure out how the disease spread; we weren't even sure if it was contagious. We didn't think so, at first. But now—"

Reed seemed to catch himself, and immediately stopped speaking. Phoebe waited for him to continue, but he had clammed up. He looked as if he was going through a silent debate over whether to tell her something.

"Now, what?" Phoebe gently pressed.

"When do you intend to run this article?" Reed asked.

Truthfully, Phoebe never intended to run the

article, but for Reed's sake, she made something up. "Early next week," she said, providing him with the most reasonable lie she could come up with. She didn't want to scare him by leading him to think that what he said was going to be in the paper the next morning. "There's no room in the weekend edition."

"And if I tell you something that hasn't been announced to the press yet, can you keep it quiet?" Reed asked. "It's something we were thinking of holding until after opening weekend, unless the situation changed."

Phoebe was intrigued about "the situation."

"I promise you, I won't write about it before you make the announcement," Phoebe said, being totally honest with him for once in their brief history.

Reed took a sip of his bottled water. "It's about Tasha."

"Tasha?"

"Our lead elephant," Reed explained. "That's another strange thing about this sickness. It always strikes the lead animal. It's as if this disease is specifically targeting the strongest and most skilled creatures."

An alarm went off inside Phoebe's head at that very moment. Here was the clue that made this illness more than a simple coincidence—something the Charmed Ones would have to look into.

"How long has Tasha been sick?" Phoebe asked.

"Her trainer noticed that she was acting sluggish two days ago," Reed said. "You can imagine that, at this point, everyone was sensitive to the signs. Tasha was immediately separated from the other animals and put in a semi-quarantine."

"Semi?"

"That means that people are free to enter her tent," Reed explained, "but she's kept away from all the other animals."

"Gotcha," Phoebe said, taking more fake notes on the page. "What else is the circus doing to protect the animals?"

"We're doing everything in our power to investigate the illness," Reed said, sounding rehearsed for the first time in the interview. "Our veterinary staff runs tests on the animals every morning. If any of them start showing signs of fatigue, they'll be immediately removed from the performing roster."

"But you haven't canceled any performances," Phoebe said.

"We employ hundreds of people," Reed explained. "And we bring in hundreds of thousands of dollars for the local economy. We can't just shut down over what could simply be a coincidence."

"A coincidence?" Phoebe wasn't buying that line of thought.

"The animals don't interact with one another," Reed said. "They all have different trainers. We haven't found anything that even links the incidents. Granted, it looks like they're connected, but we can't put all these people out of work just because it *seems* like something is going on with the animals."

"But what if more animals get sick?"

"At some point, the call will have to be made, and maybe we'll have to shut down," Reed said. "Whether the protesters believe us or not, the Fletcher Family Circus really does care about these animals as if they were family. They *are* family. Like every other member of this circus."

"I thought I heard one of the protesters say something about an investigation?"

"You did," Reed said. "And I want to make it clear that while we are looking into the situation internally, there is nothing to warrant a formal inquiry at this time."

"Still, it's an awfully big coincidence," Phoebe said. "Three animals in the same circus being struck by what seems to be the same illness."

There wasn't a doubt in Phoebe's mind that the tragedies were linked. There was even less of a question as to whether this was what Puck had sent her and her sisters to the circus to take care of for him. But she could understand why the circus people might still have their doubts. It wasn't like they were looking for a supernatural explanation.

Reed paused for a moment, considering whether it was too big of a coincidence. Phoebe was surprised when he finally responded.

"Yes. Yes, it is," he said slowly.

Chapter 11

"Thanks, Elise," Phoebe said into her cell phone. "Can you read that last part back to me?"

Phoebe listened as her boss read the final draft of her column while she waited for Paige. Since Phoebe couldn't make it back to the office, she had called Elise to go over it with her. Phoebe once again counted herself as lucky for having Elise as an editor. Few employers would put up with the unorthodox business practices and erratic hours Phoebe was forced to keep because of the demands of being a Charmed One.

It sounded like Puck had honored her request and changed her column back to the way she had originally written it. Now she would be able to turn in her column nearly on time.

"That's it," Phoebe said as Elise finished reading. "I'm glad the computer problem got fixed."

"I can't believe the tech guy didn't tell you what was wrong with it," Elise said over the phone.

"Well, he kind of did, but you know tech guys," Phoebe said. "They can be so technical." Somehow she didn't think that telling Elise that a magical prankster had hijacked her computer was a good idea. It would have led to more questions, and possibly the suggestion of some vacation time in a nice mental institution.

Now that Phoebe had dealt with the advice column, she got to the *other* purpose for the phone call. "Hey Elise, I was wondering. Have you heard about what's been going on at the circus?"

"You mean with those two animals that died?" she asked, indicating that she had heard something. "Yeah. There was some kind of press conference about it this afternoon. I didn't think there was a story there. It's unfortunate about the animals, but not really newsworthy at the moment. I'm sure the TV guys are jumping all over it because it makes for good video, but I'd prefer to wait until there's some actual proof that something is wrong. I know, call me crazy."

That was one of the things that Phoebe respected most about Elise. Sure, she could be fun and even a little irreverent at times, but she took the news very seriously. Phoebe figured that might be why Elise enjoyed working with Phoebe on her column so much. It was the one part of the paper she didn't have to stress out about. Sure, Elise was a stickler for making sure that Phoebe gave well-thought-out advice, but it wasn't the same as making sure all the facts were straight before the paper ran a piece exposing a crooked politician.

"What if I told you that another animal—an elephant—was sick?" Phoebe asked. She had debated over actually getting the paper involved, but in the end she felt that the *Mirror*'s resources could come in handy in this case.

"Well, that would be moving more in the direction of a story," Elise said. "But it still sounds like one of those TV news teasers that turns out to be a non-story. How did *you* hear about all this?"

"I met a man—"

"Sounds interesting," Elise quickly jumped in.

"Not like that," Phoebe said. Sure, they had flirted a little bit, but she was dating Jason. Sort of. "I mean, I met someone who works for the circus. You could say he kind of gave me an exclusive." *Oh, that sounded bad,* Phoebe thought.

"I'm sure he did," Elise said. "But the last time I checked, you weren't an investigative journalist."

"I don't want to step on any toes," Phoebe said. "But I just thought it was interesting."

"Well, if you want to place some calls I'm not going to stop you," Elise said. "Just don't let it interfere with your next column."

"I won't," Phoebe assured her. "I doubt it's a real story, anyway." She didn't really want the paper involved, just the paper's research department. "Do you think someone could do a quick check to see if any other reports have been filed on similar animal illnesses?"

"I'll get someone on it," Elise said. "But I'm not sure when we'll be able to get back to you. This isn't exactly a high priority."

"I appreciate whatever you can do," Phoebe said. "Thanks."

"Tell Paige to get well soon," Elise said.

"I will," Phoebe said, feeling slightly guilty about lying to her boss. She had told Elise that she was at home tending to her sister. "Bye."

"Bye."

Phoebe shut her cell phone. Once again, she was thankful that she had a boss who was so understanding. Due to her night job slaying demons, Phoebe tended to call in sick at least once a week, using one lame reason or another. It was easier to come up with excuses now that there was a baby in the house, but Phoebe hated blaming Wyatt for all her unexcused absences. There seemed something potentially karmic about telling Elise that Wyatt was sick when he was perfectly well.

At least today she had been able to use a partial truth. She had told Elise that Paige had been in a hiking accident, and then she had let Elise jump to the natural conclusion that Paige had been injured in the accident.

Phoebe had taken a calculated risk in bringing up Tasha's condition to Elise. If her editor had thought it was actually worth pursuing, she would have sent in a true journalist to cover it. In all likelihood it would have been someone Phoebe knew, and then she'd have to spend the afternoon hiding from a coworker while she continued to investigate the situation. It would have been pretty hard to come up with an explanation for why she was at the circus when she was supposed to be home taking care of Paige.

Luckily, the call had gone just as she'd expected.

Phoebe's mind was on Tasha's illness as she waited for Paige to return. They had agreed earlier to meet back at the spot where they had originally split up, by a trailer with a huge pirate flag draped on the side. In a sea of white and blue trailers, this one stood out. Phoebe briefly wondered what the flag was all about.

As she stood waiting for Paige, the clown from earlier ran by. As he hurried past Phoebe, he lifted his hat (and his wig) to her. The sight forced a smile onto her face.

At least someone is having a good day, she thought.

Phoebe was almost positive that Reed's story was the reason Puck had sent the Charmed Ones to the circus. Animals that didn't normally interact didn't just take ill and die one after another without explanation. Sure, it *could* have been a coincidence, but considering she and her sisters had been sent to the circus specifically to find an Innocent in peril, it didn't seem like that was likely.

"Hey," Paige said as she found her sister beside the pirate flag. "I think I found something."

"Me too," Phoebe said.

"Tell me on the way," Paige said, pulling her sister along.

"On the way where?" Phoebe asked.

"You'll see."

Phoebe followed as Paige guided her through the rows of empty trailers. The afternoon seemed to be taking a decidedly Nancy Drew-esque turn.

As they walked, Phoebe felt like it was starting to resemble a ghost town outside the Cow Palace. The fairgrounds were already beginning to empty as the audience made their way to their seats inside. The trailer area was also empty, as most of the circus personnel were in the staging area, prepping for the show.

Every now and then, Paige and Phoebe passed someone in costume heading for the back of the arena, but it seemed like most people were already inside. The few people they saw barely gave them a second glance.

Paige bypassed all of the trailers and went straight for the tents at the back of the restricted area. Phoebe hadn't seen this section earlier, as the taller trailers had been blocking her view. She should have assumed something like it existed. It wasn't like they were going to keep the animals in a double-wide.

About a dozen white tents of various sizes were scattered around the back section of the parking lot. This area was a little more crowded with circus staff, as the staging area for the arena was just beyond the tents.

"In here," Paige said as she checked to make sure no one was watching. She then yanked Phoebe into the last tent in the line.

A heartbreaking sight confronted Phoebe when she entered. An elephant—presumably Tasha—was lying down on her side at the center of the tent. She had never seen a sick elephant before, but this one looked quite ill.

One of Tasha's legs was chained to a spike in the ground. It seemed harsh, but Phoebe knew it was probably for the best. If Tasha was really feeling as bad as she looked, there was no telling what harm she might do to herself, or to others, without realizing it.

"Hello, girl," Paige said as she cautiously approached the pachyderm. "I told you I'd be back. And I brought my sister with me."

"Paige," Phoebe cautioned. "I don't think this is a good idea."

"Don't worry," Paige said. "She's not going to hurt me." Paige leaned down to pat Tasha on the head.

The elephant looked tired, as if she couldn't even expend the energy to raise her head. But that didn't mean Phoebe was comfortable getting close to her. One dizzy swing of the trunk could knock both Paige and Phoebe to the ground.

That was when it hit her: The trumpet sound from her premonition hadn't come from a trumpet. It had been Tasha.

The realization eliminated any lingering doubt that they had found their Innocent. *This* was the reason Puck had sent them to the circus. Now all she had to do was figure out why Puck was so concerned about the elephant.

"Don't worry, we're here to help," Paige continued, leaning in even closer to Tasha. "You're going to be fine."

"Paige," Phoebe warned again as the elephant lifted her trunk off the ground.

"It's okay," Paige said.

Phoebe watched as Tasha continued to raise her trunk, then use it to pat Paige on the arm. It was almost as if the elephant could understand what her sister was saying.

As Paige worked at soothing the savage beast, Phoebe took stock of the area. The tent was pretty much empty, except for the sick elephant. A couple of untouched hay bales sat off to the side, but nothing else was in the room.

Phoebe quickly amended her inventory when she looked up into the back corner of the tent and saw a video camera affixed to a support beam, just high enough that someone would need a ladder to change the tape.

Well, either a ladder or the power of levitation, Phoebe thought. She wondered if the video would contain anything interesting, and was about to mention it to Paige when they were unexpectedly interrupted.

"What the hell are you doing in here?" a dark-haired woman angrily asked as she came storming into the tent.

Chapter 12

"Get away from her," the woman insisted as she walked toward Paige and Tasha.

Paige stepped away from the elephant, holding up her hands. "It's okay," Paige said. "We're here to help."

"Help what?" the woman asked. "Who are you? Did Jordan call you in to consult?"

"Not exactly," Phoebe said, making a mental note to find out more about this Jordan person.

"Well then, what are you doing in here?" the woman asked again.

"Maybe we should start with introductions," Paige said. "My name is Paige Matthews. I'm with Social Services."

Phoebe looked at her sister, wondering where she was going with this. Paige hadn't worked for Social Services for several months. But, aside from that, it wasn't clear how that particular lie would help them in this situation.

"And this is Phoebe," Paige said, pointing to

her sister, but intentionally failing to provide more information.

"What does Social Services have to do with a sick elephant?" the woman asked.

"Have you noticed all the children around here?" Paige asked. "If there's some kind of epidemic hitting the circus, we need to find out as soon as possible or we're going to have to shut you down. Now, who are *you*?"

"Lane," the woman said. "Lane Strickland. I'm Tasha's trainer."

Phoebe was surprised that the cover story seemed to be working. Then again, it helped that Paige was delivering it with such conviction. It was almost as if she was daring the woman to question her reason for being there.

"Nice to meet you," Paige said, not bothering to hold out her hand. This added to the air of intimidation Paige was going for.

"A pleasure," Lane said in return, not sounding remotely like she meant it. "What were you doing with Tasha? You shouldn't have come in here unaccompanied. Tasha has been very skittish around people lately."

Phoebe found that last part interesting. Was there a cause for this newfound fear of people? Or was Lane making up an excuse to get them out of the tent? Tasha certainly seemed fine around Paige.

"Really? We seem to be getting along," Paige said, putting Phoebe's thoughts into words. It seemed to Phoebe that her sister believed the latter option to be true.

Lane bent over to give the elephant a rubdown. By the way she handled the elephant, it looked like the woman truly cared for Tasha. But that wasn't enough to convince Phoebe to cross Lane off her suspect list.

"I'm sorry, but you have to leave," Lane said. "If Social Services is truly concerned, you should speak with the circus manager. I'd be happy to point out his trailer. In the meantime, the veterinarian is on his way over to discuss putting Tasha under a full quarantine."

"Has it already gotten to that stage?" Phoebe asked.

"We think so," the woman said impatiently.

"Do you mind if I ask you one quick question?" Phoebe asked, slipping back into journalist mode.

"Yes, I do," Lane replied. "But since I get the feeling you aren't going to leave until you find out whatever it is you came for, then I guess you can ask whatever you want, so long as we go outside to do it. I don't want you bothering Tasha any more than you already have."

Phoebe and Paige reluctantly followed Lane out of the tent.

"Your question?" Lane asked once they were outside.

For a brief moment Phoebe had forgotten what she had planned to ask. She actually had three questions, but figured Lane would only give her enough time to ask one. She chose the most direct query. "Have you ever seen anything like this illness before?" Phoebe asked.

"You mean before Zeus and Sabra?" Lane asked in a condescending tone.

Phoebe nodded her head. She suspected full well that Lane knew that was what she had meant.

"No," Lane said, softening. "I've been working with animals since before I could walk. And I have never seen anything like the disease that is claiming the lives of these creatures."

"Did you notice anything odd about Tasha before she got sick?" Phoebe asked.

"I thought you said one question," Lane said, getting annoyed again.

"Please," Phoebe said.

Lane seemed to drop her guard once again, if only slightly.

"Nothing," Lane finally said. "We had a great workout the day before. Then the next morning, I came in to see her and she could barely move."

"It hit that quickly?" Phoebe asked.

"Like someone had flipped a switch," Lane said.

It sounds like someone—or something—got to Tasha, Phoebe thought.

"Thank you for your time," Paige said.

"And thank you for leaving her alone," Lane said sternly as she turned her back to them and went into the tent.

"Do you think we should wait for the vet to come by?" Paige asked.

"I think if we hang around here, Lane might sic a lion on us," Phoebe said. "We can talk to the vet later. In the meantime, I think we need to regroup."

Chapter 13

As they walked back through the trailers, Phoebe felt her cell phone vibrating in her purse. She hoped that it was Piper with some news about Puck's motives. They had found their Innocent. Now all they needed to know was how to protect her . . . and from what.

Phoebe fished inside her bag and pulled out her phone. Piper's name was flashing on the screen.

"I was just about to call you," Phoebe said as she answered.

"Finally," Piper said over the line. "I've been trying to get through to you for the past twenty minutes. Puck's been blocking my calls. Is everything okay?"

"More or less," Phoebe replied. "We haven't run into Puck since we got here—at least, I don't think we have. That's the trouble with shape-shifters; you never know when they might be lurking around."

Phoebe knew she didn't have to tell that to Piper. They'd each had plenty of experience over the years with shape-shifters, changelings, and demons that could assume other identities. Oftentimes, these entities chose to steal the identities of the Charmed Ones, which always led to complications.

"I think I know who he wants us to protect," Phoebe continued. "Can you look something up for us in the Book of Shadows?"

"Not at the moment," Piper said. "I'm at the circus."

"You're here?" Phoebe asked.

"I just came in the front gate," Piper said. "Boy, those tickets are expensive."

"I didn't think you were coming," Phoebe said.

"Leo took a break from the retreat and came home," Piper explained. "He thought I should be here. Where are you?"

"Someplace you can't enter without a pass," Phoebe said. "Hold on, I'll send Paige for you. Where should she meet you?"

"At the caramel apple stand," Piper said. "But tell her to hurry, I can feel my teeth rotting just from the smell of all this sugar."

"She's on her way," Phoebe said as she hung up the phone.

"You'll send me for her?" Paige asked. "What am I, a taxi cab?"

Phoebe rolled her eyes and told Paige where

to meet their sister. Paige gave a little wave and orbed away.

Phoebe checked her watch. The show was about to begin. That meant they had approximately two hours to solve the mystery while the circus staff was distracted by the performance. She hoped that would be enough time.

While Phoebe waited, the clown in the tiny blue bowler hat hurried past once again. He must have been late for his cue. Just like the last time, he tipped his hat—and wig—to her as he continued on his merry way.

"Oh look," she said as he passed, "a running gag."

I wonder if Puck would claim credit for that old joke too, she thought.

A moment later, Paige and Piper orbed in. Piper didn't waste time with pleasantries. "So what have we learned?"

"Well," Phoebe said, looking at Paige. "We think our Innocent's an elephant."

"An elephant?" Piper asked.

"An African elephant, to be exact," Paige added.

"I wish at least some part of this would be surprising to me," Piper said. "It makes sense, though. From what I've read, Puck has a connection to animals. Traditionally he gets along with them far better than he does with people."

"So you think he really does want us to help?" Phoebe asked.

"I don't know," Piper said. "Leo seems to think Puck may be dangerous. He wanted me to get here right away."

"Maybe he just thought any situation Puck would be involved in would be dangerous," Paige suggested. "It does seem like Puck is a pretty powerful being. He's been around since practically the beginning of time."

"All the more reason to watch out for him," Phoebe said. "Even if his intentions are good, we don't know what he's willing to do to see this thing through."

"So, what's the deal with this elephant?" Piper asked.

Her sisters quickly filled her in on what they had learned. Phoebe did most of the talking, since she had been the lead investigator, but Paige filled in the blanks with her impressions of the circus people she had observed while she was snooping.

From the snippets of conversation Paige had overheard, she deduced that the staff was trying not to jump to conclusions about the animals' illnesses, but they were all deeply concerned. Beyond worrying about their own fate if the circus closed, there seemed to be an overwhelming fear for the rest of the healthy animals. The circus employees were like a close-knit family, and they considered the animals to be members of the family unit too.

"Animals dying unexplained deaths within a

few weeks of each other?" Piper asked, summing up what she had heard. "I'd agree that that's odd, but this sounds more like a case for a trained vet than the Charmed Ones."

"There's a vet on the job already," Paige said. "But I don't think the animals are dying of natural causes."

"Why?" Piper asked.

"Well, the elephant trainer told us that she's never seen anything like it," Phoebe said. She knew that wasn't exactly hard evidence, but there was something about Lane's demeanor that had made Phoebe believe it was an important detail.

"Okay, I don't mean to be a skeptic," Piper began.

"Who are you kidding?" Paige asked lightly. "That's your main role here."

Piper shot her sister a look, but she didn't contradict her. "It still doesn't necessarily mean that there's anything supernatural going on here."

"I just have this feeling," Paige said. "Puck sent us here for a reason."

"Yeah, but we still don't know what his true goal is," Phoebe added. "If we assume he wants to help the animals, why doesn't he just do it himself? Isn't he powerful enough?"

"Why doesn't Puck just tell us what's going on?" Piper asked, though she didn't really expect an answer. "If he's really worried about the animals, what's stopping him from just saying,

'Hey, there are some sick animals at the circus. Go do something about it.'"

"He did say something about testing us," Phoebe said.

"And he did tell us to go to the circus in the first place," Paige added. "Maybe we should stop worrying about Puck and focus on the animals."

"I can do both at the same time," Piper said. "Now, if Puck sent us here to stop the animals from getting sick, I'm guessing you're right and something supernatural is the cause. We're not exactly the first people to call for medical assistance."

"We need to figure out what kind of demon is involved in this, and how it has access to the animals," Piper concluded.

"This is a pretty big circus," Phoebe said. "We've got a lot of ground to cover."

"True," Piper said. "Your new friend Reed can probably help us narrow down the list of suspects. There are only so many people who have unlimited access to all the animals."

"Good idea," Paige said.

"And you," Piper said, looking at Paige, "why don't you orb back to the Manor and look up demons that have anything to do with animals. It's safe to assume that nobody here has seen anything like this before, but it's possible our ancestors may provide us with some clues."

"Aye-aye, *mes capitaines*," Paige said, giving a mock salute.

Piper and Phoebe just stared at her for a moment.

"Anyway," Piper continued. "See what you can learn. But be quiet because Leo just put Wyatt down for a nap."

"They won't even know I'm there," Paige said as she orbed home.

"Okay," Piper said, checking her watch. "The show will be starting soon. That should make it easier for us to look around."

Just then, the clown with the tiny blue bowler hat came running up to Phoebe again. This time, he grabbed her and clutched her in an exaggeratedly romantic embrace.

"Friend of yours?" Piper asked.

The clown released Phoebe from his stranglehold, then grabbed her hand, looking for the ring he had put there earlier. He looked absolutely devastated when he saw that it was gone. To call the guy a "ham" would have been kind. Although both Phoebe and Piper were impressed when the rivers of fake tears started pouring down his face from some device he must have had hidden on his body.

"I gave it to a little girl who said she liked it," Phoebe lied, trying to stop the waterworks.

It seemed to work, because the clown perked up immediately, then suddenly took an interest in Piper. He pulled a colorful bouquet of fake flowers from his sleeve and presented them to her.

"Oh no," Piper said. "Really, I couldn't."

That set the waterworks off again.

"Take them or he'll never leave," Phoebe said to her sister through clenched teeth.

"Okay," Piper said, holding out her hand like she was accepting a soggy toy that Wyatt had been teething on. "Thank you very much."

As she took the flowers, the paper blooms immediately wilted and all the petals fell to the ground. Piper stood there for a moment, not knowing what to do.

The clown looked horrified as he quickly took the bouquet of stems back from her. Then his face fell into a look of utter sadness again. The range of emotions he had experienced in the last minute was actually pretty amazing.

"That's okay," Piper said, trying to soothe the crying clown. "But don't you have a show to—"

As soon as Piper mentioned the show, the clown went from sad to shocked and then back to horrified. It was as if he had forgotten all about the fact that the circus was about to start. Of course, it was all part of his act. Not the one onstage, but the one he was putting on for the Charmed Ones.

He checked his watch, but it only squirted more water in his face.

"We've got to find out what kind of makeup this guy uses," Phoebe said. "Talk about waterproof."

The clown grabbed one of each girl's hands

and pumped them hard, shaking good-bye. He tipped his hat to them one last time, pulling up the wig and exposing his red-and-white-colored head. Then he dashed off to the circus staging area.

Piper and Phoebe stood there gawking after him for a moment.

"So, we're thinking that was Puck, right?" Piper asked.

"Oh, yeah," Phoebe said as they started walking toward Reed's trailer.

Chapter 14

"Maybe he's watching the show," Piper suggested as Phoebe continued banging on the door to Reed's office. She had been at it for over a minute already, and still no one answered.

"Right now he's our best source of information," Phoebe said as she knocked yet again. "Our *only* source of information. Maybe he's in the back."

"Phoebe, the trailer's not that big," Piper said. "If he's in there, he's heard you knocking by now. Let's try something else."

"Everyone's in the arena," Phoebe said, looking out over the empty lot of trailers. "We might have to wait until after the show to speak with anyone."

"Ms. Halliwell?" Reed said as he popped his head out the door of the trailer that stood next door to his. "I thought I heard someone knocking. I'm not in there, by the way."

"So I gathered," Phoebe said as she and

Piper walked over to the next trailer.

"I would have thought you'd be filing your report by now," Reed said as he waved them inside. There was a slight tinge of suspicion in his voice. Phoebe couldn't blame him. He was probably wondering why she was still there.

"I had a few more questions," she said as she stepped into the media trailer. Piper was right behind her. "This is my assistant, Piper."

Piper glared at her sister for a moment, but didn't say anything.

"Nice to meet you," Reed said to Piper.

"You too," she said, shaking his hand.

The media trailer was considerably smaller than the one that served as Reed's office/living quarters. It was simply a one-room camper with a large amount of technology crammed inside. Several televisions, DVD players, and tape machines sat on a table that stretched along one wall of the tiny room. Along another wall sat shelves full of DVDs and videotapes, stacked from the floor to the ceiling. A computer, a large printer, a scanner, and a fax machine sat precariously balanced on one small console in a corner.

An air conditioner was running to keep the room cool, even though it wasn't that warm outside. Phoebe assumed that when all the machines were on, it probably got pretty hot in the small space.

"Nice setup," Phoebe said facetiously. There was barely room in the place for the three of them to stand, much less sit back and enjoy the video library.

"We do what we can in our little city on wheels," Reed said. "You should see the trailer that functions as our recreation hall. All we have in there is a game of Twister, but the trailer's so small, only one person can play at a time."

"I'm sure the contortionists must have fun," Phoebe said.

"They're undefeated," Reed said, smiling.

"That's a lot of tapes," Phoebe noted, looking at the packed shelves. She remembered the video camera in Tasha's tent and wondered if there was something in the room that might help them find the demon.

"We take videos of all the performances, dress rehearsals—practically anything related to the animals," Reed said. "We pretty much keep them under constant surveillance."

"The animal rights people would probably love to know that," Phoebe said.

"They do," Reed replied. "They're the main reason we started taping constantly. I wasn't just feeding you a line when I told you the circus cares about our animals. We want to make sure none of them are being mistreated. The video helps."

"I'm sure it does," Piper said. She was secretly hoping the recordings would help with their cause as well.

"Now, those follow-up questions?" he asked, looking back to Phoebe.

"Of course," Phoebe said as she reached into her purse and pulled out the small notepad she had stolen from him earlier. "First of all, who has access to the animals?"

"You mean, who had access to the animals before they were sick?" Reed asked.

Phoebe nodded.

"Everyone," Reed said. "Literally. You saw the fairgrounds. The animals are pretty much open to the public."

"But not while the circus is traveling," Phoebe said. She was thinking back to how Reed had said that Sabra had not taken ill until they were already on the road.

"No," Reed acknowledged. "Then it's just us circus folk. But we think that whatever bug Zeus and Sabra caught could have been incubating for days, if not weeks."

Somehow, Phoebe doubted that. She suspected that the animals had suddenly become ill, just as it appeared. "Was anyone with the animals when they died?"

"Actually, no," Reed said. "They both passed in their sleep."

"What about the video?" Phoebe asked, thinking back once again to the video camera trained on Tasha. "Did you keep them under surveillance while they were sick?"

"It's standard procedure," Reed said, "but you'd have to talk to Dr. Kahn to find out for sure."

"Jordan?" Phoebe guessed, remembering the name Lane had mentioned.

"You've met him?"

"No, but his name has come up during my investigation," Phoebe said. She noticed that Piper was casually looking over the videos on the wall. She was probably thinking the same thing as Phoebe: The tapes might show them what exactly was going on. The only problem was that Reed kept trying to include Piper in the conversation. She had to stop perusing the shelves or else he'd think she was trying to steal something.

"Investigation?" Reed asked, repeating the last word that Phoebe had used. It was clear that he wasn't pleased that her article had become an "investigation."

Phoebe didn't blame him. Lately, every time the word "investigation" was used in the news it seemed to be in reference to some overblown scandal intended to increase ratings or newspaper circulation numbers. She immediately corrected herself. "I meant *research*."

"Would Dr. Kahn keep a copy of the video in here?" Piper asked, eyeing the wall of recordings openly.

"Probably," Reed said, though he didn't offer to share the videos with them. Neither Phoebe nor Piper had expected him to—there was being helpful, and then there was risking your job.

"How long has the doctor been with the circus?" Phoebe asked.

"Oh, about a hundred years," Reed replied. "Sorry. That wasn't some kind of ageist joke. He'll be the first to tell you he's as old as the hills. But he's been here almost as long as the circus itself. He loves these animals."

"I'm sure he does," Phoebe said.

Piper threw up her hands, stopping time.

"What did you do that for?" Phoebe asked.

"This is taking too long," Piper said impatiently as she went through the tapes on the highest shelves. She had to stand on tiptoe to reach, so she couldn't have searched them while Reed was watching her. "There might be something on the tapes, and I doubt he's going to give us permission to go through them, no matter how much you flirt with him."

"I wasn't flirting," Phoebe said. "Honestly. I mean . . . I'd know if I was flirting, wouldn't I?"

Piper shot her sister a look. "You think the contortionists would have fun playing Twister? Please."

Phoebe had been certain that she had meant it innocently at the time.

"I'm sure the circus has already looked at the tapes," Phoebe said, changing the subject. "Or at least the vet probably has."

"But they wouldn't know what to look for, would they?" Piper asked. "They'd only be looking for signs of a natural cause of death."

"Technically, we don't know what to look for either," Phoebe reminded her sister.

"Yes, but we have a better chance of finding something," Piper said.

Phoebe conceded that her sister was right. "Good thinking," she said, giving in. "What do you think of the interview so far?"

"I think we're done with Reed for now. We should check out the vet," Piper replied. "I'm cautious about anyone who refers to himself as being 'old as the hills,' considering the life expectancy of a demon."

"Me too," Phoebe said. "That seems fishy."

"Possession?" Piper suggested.

"Possibly," Phoebe said. They had dealt with their fair share of demons taking over bodies in the past. In fact, demons had possessed both Piper and Phoebe at one time or another. It was possible that something similar had happened to a circus member.

Phoebe looked at her sister for a moment, as if she wanted to say something, but couldn't bring herself to do it.

"What?" Piper asked.

"Well, when I asked how you thought the interview was going, I kind of meant what did you think of my interview skills? How was I doing?"

Piper smiled. "Oh. I think you're a natural."

"Really?" Phoebe asked. "Maybe I've found a new career path."

"Yeah," Piper agreed. "But don't think that I'm going to be your assistant."

"I wouldn't," Phoebe said.

"Hey, I found something," Piper said as she pulled a pair of tapes from the top shelf. There was a rubber band holding them together. The spines read SABRA and ZEUS. "The dates on these are recent."

"The one on Sabra is the day before the circus got to San Francisco," Phoebe said, reading over Piper's shoulder. "That's the day she died."

The ringing of a cell phone interrupted their conversation. The sisters looked at each other.

"It's not mine," they said in unison.

They turned around and looked at Reed. Apparently, stopping time didn't include cellular service.

"We could let it roll over to voice mail," Phoebe suggested.

"I think we've got what we need," Piper said as they moved back into the positions they were in before she had frozen time. Piper handed her sister the tapes so Phoebe could slip them into her purse. The black cases barely managed to fit inside the small bag.

Piper gave a wave of her hands, and time resumed as Reed's cell phone continued to ring.

Reed was caught off-guard by the noise coming from his phone. "Excuse me," he said as he pulled it out of the holster hooked onto his belt. "Reed here," he said into the phone.

A moment later, Phoebe's cell phone rang as well.

"Maybe it's contagious," Piper joked as Phoebe answered the phone.

It was Elise. Apparently, an intern had managed to track down the information Phoebe had asked for earlier.

Phoebe jotted down what Elise told her on her stolen notepad. It was very interesting, to say the least. It also added a whole new level to the seriousness of the situation.

As Phoebe finished taking her notes, she glanced up and could tell by the look on Reed's face that his conversation was just as serious as hers. They both hung up their phones at the same time.

"Is there a problem?" Phoebe asked. She happened to look past him at a calendar posted on the wall. It was a mini-poster listing the circus's tour dates from the past year.

"Dr. Kahn has just put Tasha under full quarantine," Reed said. "I'm afraid things aren't looking good."

"I'm so sorry," Phoebe said, shooting her sister a look.

Piper got the message. She shifted to the side of the trailer so that Reed was between the two of them. "Is there anything we can do?" Piper asked, drawing his attention away from Phoebe.

"Just put together a fair article," he said, with a touch of sadness.

"We wouldn't think of doing anything else," Phoebe said a second after she slipped the calendar into her waistband.

"If you'll excuse me," Reed said as he ushered Piper and Phoebe out of the trailer.

"I was still hoping to ask you some more questions," Phoebe said, trying to find a reason to stay in the trailer with the video equipment. They needed to watch the tapes she had stolen.

"Please, stay and watch the show," Reed said, referring to the circus, not the pilfered videos, as he walked them outside. He pulled a handful of comp tickets from his inside jacket pocket.

"Thanks," Phoebe said, looking at the tickets. "But there are only two of us." She figured it would be best not to mention Paige at the moment. He didn't need to know that there were three people on the case.

"They're general comps," Reed explained. "You can come back with your families. Or your boyfriends."

Phoebe blushed, and didn't bother to mention that her boyfriend was currently half a world away.

"But use two now," Reed continued. "We'll be issuing a statement about Tasha after the performance. Feel free to stick around until then."

"Okay," Phoebe said reluctantly as she took the tickets and followed him down the steps with Piper. She knew they weren't about to waste time watching the show right now, but they could always come back later, depending on how the day turned out.

"Give our best to Tasha," Piper added.

Reed left them with a sad smile as he went off toward the tents.

"So what now?" Piper asked.

"Look at this," Phoebe said as she pulled out the calendar, holding it up so her sister could see what it was. "That was Elise on the phone. Apparently there have been similar animal deaths occurring at zoos across the country."

"And no one has noticed this before?"

"It was happening to different animals at different zoos," Phoebe said as she held the calendar next to the notes she had taken from Elise. "Who would notice a sick rhinoceros in Houston and then a sick monkey in Santa Fe? There didn't seem to be anything in common except—"

"Except that the animals were dying in the cities the circus visited," Piper finished.

"About one animal a month," Phoebe said, consulting the calendar. "Or sometimes every other month. Until Las Vegas, that is. There weren't any deaths reported in zoos in Las Vegas, San Diego, or Los Angeles."

"And then the circus animals started being affected," Piper surmised. "Two died, and one took ill within the span of a couple of weeks."

"So whenever the zoo killings ended, the circus deaths began," Phoebe said as she looked over the calendar.

"So, what's our next move?" Piper asked, pushing aside the newest revelation for the moment.

"I guess I can interview the vet when Reed is done with him," Phoebe suggested. "Until then, we can try to find a way to break into the media trailer and check out the tapes."

"Or we could just wait for Paige," Piper suggested.

"Wait for Paige for what?" the third Charmed One asked as she orbed in beside her sisters.

"You up for a little breaking and entering?" Phoebe asked.

"Always," Paige said with a devilish grin.

Chapter 15

Blue and white orbs filled the media trailer as the Charmed Ones materialized in the locked room. Even though Piper and Phoebe had been inside the trailer a minute earlier, the place seemed to have gotten even smaller since they'd left.

"Man, it's tight in here," Paige said as she released her sisters' hands. "We're lucky I didn't orb us into the table."

"Sorry," Piper said. "We should have warned you."

The sisters moved away from one another to give themselves some breathing room.

"Here you go," Phoebe said as she pulled the tape cases out of her purse and handed them to Piper, who was closest to the A/V equipment.

Piper looked at the collection of televisions and video players. She pushed the power button on the nearest TV, but nothing happened. She got the same response from every television in the row.

"Well, that's weird," Piper said when she couldn't get the video players to work either.

"Maybe the power's disconnected?" Paige suggested.

"I think this has something to do with the problem," Phoebe said, pointing to a small metal box that was clamped on to the end of the table.

Piper examined the box. It appeared to be a touch screen with various buttons that apparently controlled the televisions and the video and DVD players. It was ridiculously complex and seemed utterly pointless, considering the machines were only a few feet away, and Piper figured it would have been much easier to turn the machines on individually instead of by this bizarre remote. "Any idea how this thing works?" she asked as she stood over the controller.

The silence in the small room gave Piper her answer.

"Okay," Piper said as she examined the controller. "While I try to figure this out, Paige, tell us what you learned."

"I think we have our perp," she said triumphantly. "It's called a Bestiari Demon. Its M.O.—"

"'M.O.'?" Phoebe said.

"'Modus operandi,'" Paige explained.

"I know what it stands for," Phoebe said. "But when did you start talking like you're on a cop show? 'Perp'? 'M.O.'?"

"Sorry," Paige said. "I've been watching too much TV lately. But you have to admit, this is kind of like one of those procedurals—lining up the suspects and trying to make one of them talk. I think it's kind of fun."

"At least someone's enjoying herself," Piper said as she pressed a button. She was rewarded with a video player coming to life. "You were saying?"

"Bestiari Demon," Paige repeated. "It's a demon in human form that drains life-energy from animals."

"Any chance we have a specific description of the human form this demon takes?" Piper asked. The Book of Shadows was often quite helpful in describing demons for the Charmed Ones. Color drawings often accompanied the passages from some of their more artistically inclined ancestors.

"Sorry," Paige said. "There wasn't a picture available. But I do know he's male, for what that's worth."

"Was there anything in there about possession?" Phoebe asked. "Could the Bestiari Demon be forcing someone else to approach the animals for him?"

"Nope," Paige said. "It sounds like he needs to absorb the energy directly into his body."

"Well, that knocks Lane off the suspect list," Phoebe mused. "But that still leaves dozens of circus staffers with Y chromosomes."

"What does the demon do with this life-energy?" Piper asked.

"He collects it," Paige said. "And then he uses it to make himself stronger. The more power he absorbs, the more powerful he gets. And he starts to adapt the animals' attributes as well."

"So we're talking about a demon with the strength of a tiger, a horse, and an elephant?"

"And all the other animals from the zoos across the country," Phoebe added. "We don't know how many animal spirits he's collected. Or how powerful he has become." Phoebe quickly filled Paige in on what they had learned about the circus tour schedule matching the dates and locations of the zoo deaths.

"But that still doesn't explain why he stopped attacking animals in the zoos and moved on to the circus," Piper said. "It doesn't make any sense that he would go after animals that were all in one place. It would be too easy for people to notice what was happening."

"Maybe the demon didn't have a choice," Phoebe suggested. "Maybe the Bestiari doesn't just collect the animal spirits and strength as a fun pastime. It's possible that he needs to do this to live. He's been traveling with the circus so he can go from town to town without being noticed, and all the while he has a fresh supply of animals on hand in case of an emergency."

"But there are animals all over the place,"

Piper said. "Why does he need to confine his attacks to zoos and the circus?"

Phoebe was using her newly developed journalistic instincts to pull together the story. It was exciting to see how all the pieces fit into place. She thought about writing a real article for practice. Not that she'd be able to show it to anyone, of course, since it would be about a demon attack.

"Because that's where the biggest and strongest animals are," Phoebe said. "Tigers, elephants. Maybe it's like a drug. As he collects more spirits, he needs increasingly more powerful animals to keep feeding his need. Rats and sparrows don't give him the same boost anymore."

"And when he wasn't able to feed off the zoo animals in Las Vegas or San Diego—for whatever reason—he was probably going through some serious withdrawal by the time he got to Los Angeles," Piper reasoned. "Which is why he's attacked three animals in such a short time span."

"You'd think he'd just move to Africa," Paige said.

"And give up the circus life?" Phoebe replied. She tried to wrap her head around the fact that the Bestiari Demon was living among the circus folk. It was beginning to look like everything she had read or seen in the movies about circus workers being a tight-knit family was true. It was hard to imagine that one of them was a demon secretly living among them. Then again, her coworkers at the paper would probably be just as surprised to learn that there was a witch working among them.

"Then, is Tasha beyond saving?" Phoebe asked. "Has the demon already drained her life-essence and now it's just a matter of time before she dies?"

"No," Paige said. "It takes three attempts for the demon to fully drain an animal's life-force. Each time, the animal will get weaker, but it isn't fatal until the transfer of power is complete. But the Bestiari won't have access to Tasha's strength until she's dead. It's sort of kept in reserve until the final draining is absolutely complete."

"But still, that's one powerful demon," Phoebe said.

"Wait," Paige said. "Remember, it gets worse. The Bestiari doesn't just take an animal's strength, he also takes its abilities."

"So it's a *really* powerful demon," Phoebe said.

"And it's possible that he can camouflage himself like a chameleon and use any number of defensive techniques that exist in the animal world," Paige added.

"Any clues on how to vanquish it?" Piper asked.

"A Power of Three spell," Paige replied, simply.

"That's it?" Piper asked. She was still figuring out the controls to the televisions. She'd inserted the first of the tapes into the functioning tape player, but the television screens were still blank. On the bright side, she was halfway there.

"Have I missed something?" Paige asked. "Isn't the Power of Three the most kick-butt thing in our arsenal?"

"Of course," Phoebe said, ignoring her sister's "kick-butt" phraseology. "Piper just meant that it seems a little anticlimactic. Puck pulled us into this thing to test us. He's pit us against a crazy powerful demon. I would have thought there would be more to the solution."

"Nope," Paige said. "Just the Power of Three."

"Well, I'm not going to complain," Piper said. "Besides, I think I've got this thing figured out." She pushed one last button on the control unit, and the five TV screens in the small trailer came to life simultaneously.

"I think one screen would be enough," Phoebe said.

"You figure out how to turn on just one and we'll use it," Piper said. "In the meantime, I'm ready to watch a movie." She pressed play on the control.

It took a moment for the image to kick in, then the blank blue screens on each of the five TVs were replaced with blackness again. But this time, it wasn't the emptiness of an inactive TV screen, it was the darkness of a recording taken in a room with no lighting.

"Well, this is useless," Phoebe mumbled.

After about ten seconds of empty air, a spotlight cut into the middle of the screen. It revealed a man dressed like a ringmaster, standing in the center ring of—presumably—a three-ring circus. Most likely, the Fletcher Family Circus.

The ringmaster wasn't in a dark room. He was in a huge, darkened arena. Behind the ringmaster, the outline of the audience could be seen. This was definitely not a recording of Zeus's last night of life.

"Ladies, gentlemen, and children of all levels of maturity," the ringmaster said, "welcome to the Fletcher Family Circus."

"Look," Paige said as she pointed to the date burned into the upper-right-hand corner of the screen. If it was correct, it meant that the recording had been made more than a year ago. It was unlikely that this tape had anything to do with the death of the tiger.

"That doesn't match the date on the outside of the case," Piper said.

"Fast-forward," Phoebe said. "Let's see the tiger act."

Piper pushed a button and sent the images scanning forward.

"I'm no film expert, but for some reason, I don't think this is the right tape," Piper said.

She hit play when the tiger act came on.

Whoever had been operating the video camera had had a good position to catch all the action that was taking place in the center ring. The tiger tamer was putting the animals through their paces in a large cage. Each of the tigers was running up and down ladders, crossing bridges, and jumping through hoops.

As far as the Charmed Ones could tell, there wasn't anything out of the ordinary about the performance. Zeus was obviously the star of the show. He was the largest of the tigers and performed the most challenging tricks by far, receiving the lion's share of both the spotlight and the applause.

There didn't seem to be anything suspicious about what was on screen. The tiger looked perfectly healthy, which made sense since he wouldn't get sick until about ten months after the performance they were watching, assuming the date on the screen was to be believed.

"Look for the case with this date on it," Piper suggested as she ejected the tape out of the machine and slid the one marked SABRA in its place.

Paige, being closest to the wall of tapes, confirmed the date and began searching through the rows of cases. Since the tapes were in chronological order, it wasn't hard to find the one she was looking for. It was on the third row, near the center.

While Piper once again fiddled with the

media center controls, Paige opened the tape case. It was empty. She showed her sisters, who were disappointed, though not surprised, by the discovery.

Piper hit play to start the Sabra tape. The three sisters were treated to yet another circus opening. This one was dated the day after the date posted on the previous tape. While she fast-forwarded to the horse act, Paige pulled the corresponding tape case from the wall and opened it. That case was empty as well.

The horse act was just as useless as the tiger act in the previous tape. Sabra went through her routine flawlessly. She seemed strong and vibrant, with nary a stumble as she circled the area, bowed to the audience, and reared up on her hind legs. There was nothing at all to indicate that she would be dead within the year.

"This is getting us nowhere," Piper said. "The tapes have obviously been switched."

"Do you think the Bestiari knows we're investigating?" Paige asked.

"Maybe," Phoebe said. "And maybe the demon thought to cover his tracks."

Piper hit the stop button and ejected the second tape. The television screens went blue for a moment, then they burst into a crazy swirl of colors. It was like the televisions had all decided to go on a psychedelic trip together. Once the trip ended, each of the screens displayed a full-size image of Puck's face.

"Good morning, Angels," the face said with a giddy grin.

"What?" Piper asked.

"I said, 'Good morning, Angels,'" Puck repeated. "Now you're supposed to say, 'Good morning, Charlie.' Come on, let's do it again."

His image blinked off the screen for a moment, then reappeared on the televisions, without the preceding light show this time.

"Good morning, Angels," Puck said.

The Charmed Ones just stared at him.

"You three are no fun," Puck said. "You have no appreciation for the classics. I can't even get a simple 'Good morning, Charlie.'"

Piper checked her watch. "It's after noon."

"And correct me if I'm wrong," Phoebe said, "but in that particular classic, the one pulling the strings was heard, but never *seen*."

"Touché," Puck said, before changing the subject. "I was just dropping by for a progress report. How are we doing? Have we solved the mystery and saved the day yet?"

"You've got to be kidding," Piper said. It was one thing to be going along with his little test. It was quite another to have to report to him as if they were his employees.

"Come on, come on, come on," Puck said, tapping his finger against the television screen from the inside as if he were actually physically encased in the sets. "Time is money."

The Charmed Ones looked at one another,

confused.

"I take it you've found your Innocent?" Puck asked, trying to pull the information from them.

"Like you don't already know," Phoebe said.

"And what are we doing to protect her?" he asked from the TV screens. His tone was like that of a kindergarten teacher talking down to his students.

"We're trying to find out who had access to Tasha," Phoebe said, drawing a look from her sisters. "What? He's not going to go away until we tell him something."

Piper shook her head, accepting what her sister had said. "We've got some suspects," she finally said, using Paige's cop lingo. "But there are too many people with access to the animals to narrow down the list."

Puck stared blankly at the Charmed Ones for a beat. "You do realize you're dealing with a demon?" he asked, still using his condescending tone. "It's not like you can put him in a lineup and point him out among the humans. It doesn't work that way."

Piper rolled her eyes. "We're not amateurs," she said, then rattled off what they already knew. "It's a Bestiari Demon. It can take human form. And if we can stop him before he visits Tasha again, we can save her."

"Well, at least you've gotten that far on your own," Puck said. "I was beginning to worry. But just because the demon can take human form doesn't automatically mean that it uses human ways to do things. Now stop clowning around and live up to those reputations that have gotten the Underworld buzzing."

Without another word from Puck, all the TV screens changed to a test pattern, with the National Anthem playing softly in the background.

"'Stop clowning around'?" Phoebe said indignantly. "Who is he kidding?"

"I hate to say it, but he's got a point," Paige said. "A demon doesn't need permission to visit the animals. The Bestiari probably manages to come and go as it pleases."

"True," Piper said. "But if the demon has been traveling with the circus in his human form, he would still be using human means to do *some* things. Either way, his image would be on a recording from the nights the animals died. If we find those tapes, we'll find our demon."

Chapter 16

Since it was less suspicious to be seen walking out of the media trailer than orbing out of it, the Charmed Ones chose the mortal way to make their exit. Piper was the first one out, and she made sure the area was clear before her sisters exited. There was no need to bring any unwanted attention to themselves—aside from the fact that they didn't want to get kicked out of the circus, they also didn't want to alert the demon that they were onto him. Phoebe made sure that the trailer door locked behind them so no one would know they had been inside.

Once they were back out on the grounds, they paused to take stock of their surroundings yet again. Rows and rows of trailers were laid out all around them. And maybe somewhere in those trailers were two tapes that could potentially lead them to their demon. All they had to do was find them.

"How are we supposed to find two tapes in all these trailers?" Paige wondered.

"And who's to say they haven't been destroyed already?" Phoebe added bleakly.

"Wait a minute," Piper said. "We don't have to find those specific tapes. Reed had indicated that there was a *copy* of the recordings in the media trailer."

"Which would mean that the veterinarian probably still has the originals," Phoebe surmised.

"Unless, of course, the veterinarian is the demon," Piper noted.

"One scenario at a time," Phoebe said. "First thing's first. We need to check the vet's trailer for the tapes."

"I think I saw his trailer back by the tents," Paige said.

"Good," Phoebe said. "Because I think I see the vet coming this way."

Phoebe nodded toward the end of the long row of trailers. Reed was coming their way, accompanied by a man wearing a white lab coat. Although the circus apparently employed a small team of veterinarians, Phoebe suspected that this was the man they were looking for. As Reed had described earlier, the veterinarian looked ancient. He also seemed surprisingly spry for someone that old.

"Okay. New plan," Piper said. "Phoebe, you intercept Reed and Kahn. While you interview the vet, Paige and I will sneak into his trailer and see what we can find."

"I don't know," Paige said. "I think we should stay together. The Book of Shadows said we'd need the Power of Three to stop this demon."

"We can't stop the demon until we know what it looks like," Piper reasoned. "And it will be faster to find that out if we split up."

"If you think that's the way to go . . . ," Paige said, not convinced.

Piper and Paige hurried off toward the back row of trailers before Reed could see them. The last thing Phoebe needed was to cause Reed concern, and if he thought that the story was so large that the paper had sent in an entire team of investigators, he would certainly panic.

Phoebe tried to look casual and indifferent as Reed and the veterinarian approached, as if she had just been hanging around waiting for the press release he had promised her after the show. She suspected that she wasn't quite pulling it off, since Reed looked like he was bracing himself for another round of questions as he and the doctor walked up to her. For a moment she thought he was going to blow her off, pretending as if he hadn't seen her.

That was when Phoebe realized the full power of the press. Even though she and Reed seemed to have been getting along fairly well, she obviously made him nervous about what

she could uncover. Phoebe thought his skittish-
ness was a little suspicious. Beyond trying to
cover up the circus's secret animal problem,
maybe he had another secret that was worth
hiding.

"Ms. Halliwell, I thought you'd be inside
enjoying our show," Reed said. He didn't sound
too disappointed to see her. Maybe she had been
reading too much into his concerned expression.

"Please. It's Phoebe," she said, directing a
smile at both men. "I was hoping to get some
more information on Tasha. Maybe some more
colorful background, to make her real for the
readers. If we get this story out, somebody
might recognize what's happening to her and
offer some assistance."

"I'd take help from anyone," the veterinarian
said. "At this point, the only thing I haven't tried
is looking up Dr. Dolittle."

Reed quickly made the introductions,
explaining that Phoebe was a reporter for the
Bay Mirror.

"You wouldn't have time for some questions,
would you, Doctor?" Phoebe asked.

"Love to, love to, and please call me Jordan,"
Dr. Kahn replied. "Just as long as Reed here
approves. I don't talk to anyone without his permission."

"Jordan, I've told you a hundred times, you
can give interviews whenever you want," Reed
said, with fake exasperation in his voice. "All

you have to do is let me know you're doing it. I think it would be great for you to speak with Phoebe."

"Isn't it nice how encouraging he is?" Jordan asked.

"He's a sweetheart," Phoebe said.

"Have I mentioned that Dr. Kahn is a bit of a matchmaker?" Reed asked as he moved toward his trailer. "Why don't you do the interview in here? Then the doctor and I can get straight to work on the press release afterward."

"Perfect. How is Tasha doing?" Phoebe asked as the three of them went inside. Considering that she had visited the elephant earlier, she was fairly certain she already knew the answer to that question.

Jordan took a seat on the couch, patting the cushion beside him for Phoebe to sit down. The small couch seemed rather tight for the two of them to sit together, but Phoebe went along with it. She figured she'd get more out of him if they developed a comfortable rapport.

Once Phoebe was seated, the veterinarian answered her question. As he spoke, his jovial attitude evaporated. "She's not well, Phoebe. Not well at all. She could leave us at any moment."

Phoebe wondered if he knew just how accurate his words really were. From the way Tasha looked, she could tell that all it was going to take was one more visit from the Bestiari. Phoebe and her sisters needed to find a way to keep that from happening. Luckily, she knew that Lane was with the elephant now, so the Bestiari wouldn't go near Tasha. But time was running out.

She took her stolen notepad out of her purse and once again adopted the persona of a seasoned reporter. Phoebe knew she had to finesse her way into finding out about the demon and the missing tapes. She couldn't just ask the vet point-blank.

After several arbitrary questions about the nature of the animals' illnesses, Phoebe started to feel bad for the doctor. He obviously loved the animals and was taking the illnesses, and the fact that he hadn't been able to help Zeus, Sabra, or Tasha, hard.

The problem was that so far, Phoebe felt empathetic toward *everyone* she had spoken to about Tasha and the other animals. If this continued, she was going to have a hard time maintaining her journalistic objectivity. Even worse, if everyone continued to come off as completely devastated over the loss of the animals, it was going to make it nearly impossible to determine who among them was the killer.

"I just don't know what I could have done differently," Jordan lamented.

Phoebe wished she could explain to him that he had done nothing wrong; that the cure was entirely out of his hands. But of course Phoebe couldn't explain that the illness was more super than natural without revealing her identity as a Charmed One. Besides, if she did tell them, they'd probably think she was a nut and Reed would probably have her escorted off the property. He might even call the *Mirror*.

Reed had taken a seat at his desk and was busying himself with some work, but it was clear that he was listening to everything they said and was ready to jump in, if necessary. Phoebe didn't get the feeling that he was trying to stifle the story so much as protect his friend in case the questioning started to get too intense.

Phoebe finally got down to the real questions.

"How long have you been with the circus?" she asked. Though the doctor's words had been moving, she and her sisters had fallen for manufactured acts of grief before. Considering his unlimited access to the animals, Dr. Kahn should technically be at the top of their suspect list.

"Oh, about a hundred years now," he replied.

Phoebe caught Reed's eye, and the two shared a smile. Apparently, the vet was more than willing to joke about his longevity.

"And you've never seen anything like this before?" Phoebe asked.

"Well, now, I never said that, did I?" the doctor replied.

Phoebe forgot her notepad for the moment. No one—not Lane, not Elise—had mentioned

any unexplained illnesses striking the circus animals before.

"So this *has* happened before?" Phoebe asked.
Even Reed looked surprised.

"Once," Jordan said. "It must have been . . .
well . . . several years ago. Before Reed over
there started with us, I think. I could be wrong
about that—it's tough for me to keep the years
straight anymore."

Phoebe smiled sympathetically at the doctor,
but her mind was still focused on his revelation.
Reed didn't offer any indication as to whether he
knew what year the doctor was talking about.
He just sat quietly and listened along with
Phoebe.

"Anyway," Jordan continued, "the circus usually takes the winter months off from performing. That's a throwback to when we used to do
everything back in a real big top, in the great out-
doors. Nowadays, we can keep the animals—
and ourselves—in warm, climate-controlled
buildings and pens so we don't need to worry
that much about the weather beyond how it
affects our ability to get us from one place to the
other."

"I see," Phoebe said, not really sure where
this was going.

"So, it was our last show, and we were in
Denver," Jordan said. "Which is poor planning,
if you ask me. Who books a gig in the moun-
tains so late in the year? But that was . . . oh . . .

about half a dozen booking agents ago."

Phoebe liked the elderly man's detailed conversational style, but she was beginning to wonder if he was ever going to get to the point.

"So, there's this massive snowstorm," he continued. "It totally closed down the city, and the circus was trapped. Roads were closed. Everything was shut down. And this was in Denver! A city that knows how to deal with snow, not someplace that gets a snowstorm once every few years. So you know it had to be big. We couldn't get out for days, and while we were waiting for the routes to clear, Tongo took ill."

"Tongo was the circus's lead elephant before Tasha," Reed explained. "He was retired the year before I started here."

"Retired?" Phoebe asked. "So Tongo survived?"

"Yes," Jordan replied. "He got really sick, too. He looked much like Tasha does today. We were afraid to move him, but once we got the go-ahead from the weather service, we were on the road. Tongo was completely cured by the time we stopped for a rest in Salt Lake City."

Phoebe knew if the newspaper's staff had looked back far enough, they would have found an animal death in Salt Lake that would have coincided with the circus's arrival. She took Tongo's story as confirmation of what she and Piper already suspected. The Bestiari Demon must have been forced to feed off a circus animal while stuck in Denver. But the first opportunity he had to find an animal outside of the circus, he took it. Obviously it was safer not to feed where he lived.

Of course, that confirmation did nothing to help locate the demon today. It did, however, tell her that the demon had been around even longer than she had suspected. Considering the number of animals it had lived off of, she suspected that it was possibly one of the strongest demons the Charmed Ones had ever encountered.

No wonder Puck didn't want to deal with the demon on his own, she thought.

"Reed mentioned that Tasha is under full quarantine?" Phoebe asked.

"We had to do it," Jordan said. "I don't think humans are susceptible to this illness. I'm more worried for Tasha's sake. We don't need a bunch of well-intentioned folk coming by to see her in her final hours. We need to give the girl some rest."

"So who *is* allowed in the tent?" Phoebe asked.

"Her trainer and I," Jordan said, shifting in his seat. "That's it. We don't even let the head of the circus in. Reed here was the last unauthorized person to see her before we sealed up her area."

Phoebe thought she had caught something unsaid in the way the vet shifted his body. Maybe she *was* developing journalistic instincts. "If you'll pardon me for saying, you don't seem very sure about that. Are you positive no one else could get inside to see Tasha?"

"No, that's all," Reed said. "The circus is very clear about this policy."

But Phoebe could tell that while the circus may have been clear, Jordan was not.

"Dr. Kahn," Phoebe said, gently. "Jordan. Someone else has been visiting the animals, right?"

The doctor seemed to mull over the question. Phoebe could tell that he didn't want to lie to her.

"I promise whatever you tell me about this visitor will not be included in the article," Phoebe said. Considering that there wasn't going to be any article, it was an easy promise to make. "I can't imagine that it's important to the story, but now you've piqued my curiosity."

"If you say it won't go any further than this trailer, I guess there's no harm in telling you," Jordan said. "It's just, he loves the animals so much. I couldn't bear to keep him away from them in their final hours."

"So you let someone visit the animals with you?" Phoebe guessed.

"No, never with me," Jordan said. "The circus managers are really strict about these things, so I can't just go walking in with whoever strikes my fancy. But I usually give the guard permission to let the animals have a visitor when no one is around—you know, at night. . . ."

"So there's a good chance this person was

with Zeus and Sabra when they died?" Phoebe asked.

Jordan nodded his head. "But he didn't do anything to them. Tommy couldn't have been responsible for this illness."

"Tommy?" Phoebe asked, latching on to the name that Jordan had dropped.

"Tommy Brace," Jordan said. "He's been with the circus for years. I know he's going to be torn up when I tell him that he can't go in to see Tasha. But the guys in the front office are really tightening the reigns, what with it looking like a mini-epidemic is sweeping the circus. I don't want to risk us both getting in trouble."

"I don't think I've met Tommy yet," Phoebe said, hoping to wrangle an introduction.

"You wouldn't know him by that name," Reed said as he opened up a circus program and handed it to her. "But you may recognize him."

Phoebe looked at the photo and was shocked to realize that she *had* met Tommy Brace. She had met him a few times, in fact.

At the very end of the last row of trailers, Piper and Paige were conducting their own investigation. Paige had orbed them into Dr. Kahn's trailer. It had been easy to get around since the entire circus staff was busy with the performance.

"This isn't good," Paige said as they took in the sight of the trailer around them. "The place has been ransacked."

Unlike Reed's trailer, this one was entirely devoted to living space. The overall design made sense to Piper. After all, the vet didn't need an office. It wasn't like he was going to be seeing his patients in his trailer.

"I don't think so," Piper said as she looked at the mess.

Clothes and books and all sorts of junk were strewn about the place haphazardly. But it didn't seem to have been done with any set goal in mind. The furniture wasn't turned over. The few drawers and cabinets in the place were all closed. They hadn't been flung open and left hanging about as if someone had done a hurried search of the quarters.

The stack of dirty dishes in the sink and the overflowing trash can cinched it for Piper. No one had torn through the place searching for the tapes. The veterinarian was simply a slob.

"I don't think we have to worry," Piper said. "Just consider the place 'lived in.'"

Though the state of the trailer would help cover up their own search, it also hindered their ability to actually find anything. It took close to five minutes for them to even locate the thirteen-inch TV set the doctor kept in his residence. It was under an overturned box that he had obviously used as his breakfast table. From there they had to follow the cable leading to the tape player that had been shoved under the couch on the other side of the room.

There was still a tape lodged inside the machine. Piper just hoped that it wasn't anything from the veterinarian's personal collection. Luckily, when she hit play she was greeted with an image of what looked to be a very sick tiger lying in a cage.

"He must have been watching this while going over Tasha's case," Paige said.

"Lucky for us, because I don't know how we would have found the tape in here otherwise," Piper said as she watched the tape, keeping a sharp eye out for anything out of the ordinary.

"Everything looks fairly routine, so far," Paige said as they scanned through the images that zipped across the screen in fast-forward motion. It was dark inside the tiger's tent, and Zeus was lying in his cage. He wasn't moving, and it was hard to tell if he was asleep or already dead.

Piper watched with her hand on the remote control. That had been a lucky find, as well—it had been sitting on top of the machine, under the couch. "This has got to be the—"

"Stop," Paige said. "Go back."

Piper hit the buttons on the remote control, taking the images back several frames, and then hit play. Together, she and Paige watched as a shape entered the darkened tent.

"Who is that?" Piper asked.

It was difficult to see the person on the dark screen. It was clearly a man—or a demon-man.

They could tell by the way he carried himself. There was something slightly off about him, though. The shadows of his body seemed odd. It was like he was wearing some kind of disguise to hide his true features. His head seemed too big, and his clothes were too large for his frame.

The man crept silently toward the cage. Piper stood up as the man leaned into the cage and reached in for Zeus. She was transfixed by what she was watching. It was hard enough to make out any details in the darkness, but it was impossible to tell what he was doing to the tiger because his back was to the camera.

If only the camera had been positioned in the opposite direction, they would have gotten a clear shot of the demon illuminated by the red glow. But they were only able to make out his silhouette, since he stood between the light and the camera. Yet there was something oddly familiar about the outline of his overly large body.

After about a minute, the man stood up and backed away from the cage. Piper didn't have to see the tiger to know that Zeus was dead. When the demon turned to face the camera, he became much easier to identify.

Piper thought it was weird that the man would be in costume in the middle of the night, but it certainly wasn't the strangest thing she had seen in her ongoing battle with demons. It took a moment to make out his full features, but there was no mistaking the tiny bowler hat on his crazy-wigged head.

They had found their demon.

Chapter 17

"Do you have a photo of Tommy without his makeup?" Phoebe asked as she tried to recover from the shock of her discovery. She didn't want them to think anything was out of the ordinary since she could never even begin to explain what was going on. The clown in the tiny blue bowler hat was staring back at her from the full-color photo in the program with the name TOMMY BRACE printed underneath.

"I don't think I've ever seen him without makeup on," Jordan said. He looked to Reed, who shook his head, indicating that he'd never seen the clown's real face either.

"He's *always* in costume?" Phoebe asked.

"Around here, anyway," Jordan said. "I don't know how he dresses on his own time. What he chooses to wear after he leaves the circus grounds is his business, as far as I'm concerned."

"As I said, we take the circus very seriously around here," Reed added.

Phoebe suspected Tommy's costume obsession had more to do with the ability to go about unnoticed than dedication to his job. She was mentally kicking herself for not catching on to Tommy earlier. One of her favorite old movies was *The Greatest Show on Earth.* In it, Jimmy Stewart's character was wanted for murder, but he managed to hide in plain sight by working as a clown who never removed his makeup.

Phoebe thanked the veterinarian for the information, without letting on just how helpful he had been. As she left the trailer, Reed promised her that the press release about Tasha's illness would be available soon. Phoebe silently hoped that by the time the document was available she and her sisters would have vanquished the demon and Tasha would be on the road to recovery. To do that, she needed to find her sisters.

Paige had mentioned that she had seen the veterinarian's trailer back by the tents. That wasn't a surprise, since he'd want to be as close to the animals as possible. Phoebe had considered asking Jordan for directions in case she wanted to stop by later with some follow-up questions, but she thought it might make Reed suspicious.

Phoebe headed toward the back row of trailers, reading the nameplates as she walked. Either she had missed a nameplate or she had started on the wrong row, because Phoebe reached Tasha's tent without seeing Jordan's trailer.

She was just about to turn back and look

through the trailers again when she had the feeling that something was out of place. It wasn't quite a premonition, but she got a strange vibe from the tent. It took her a second, but she soon realized what was amiss. There was a big quarantine sign on the outside of the tent wall, but no sign of any kind of security to keep anyone from entering. Jordan had specifically mentioned a security guard had been posted at the tent.

He had also said that the tent was sealed. Though Phoebe didn't think that it would be airtight, it was odd that the entryway stood wide open.

Since the circus staff was otherwise occupied, Phoebe took the absence of a security guard as an open invitation to check on Tasha. Even though her inner voice was telling her to find her sisters first, Phoebe didn't listen. She had a bad feeling that the lack of a guard meant that something was definitely wrong. The sooner she found out what was going on, the better.

Phoebe cautiously entered the tent and found the crazy clown from earlier kneeling on the ground, with his hands on Tasha's side. He was even less funny now that Phoebe knew he was the Bestiari Demon.

A nearly imperceptible red glow was emanating from his fingers, and his eyes were closed as he stole the life-essence from the pachyderm. Phoebe worried that alone she was no match for such a strong demon, but she couldn't simply stand back and watch Tasha die. "Hey, Tommy," she said. "I've come to give back your ring."

The Bestiari Demon's eyes snapped open. He looked shocked to see her standing there. Phoebe wasn't sure if that was because he had recognized her as one of the Charmed Ones or if he was just startled at the presence of another person. She hoped that it was the latter. At least that would give her the element of surprise.

The demon's eyes were glowing red. Clearly, he did not like his work interrupted. He snarled at Phoebe like one of the wild animals he had inside of him. Phoebe followed his gaze as he looked down at Tasha. The elephant's breathing was labored, but she was still alive.

Phoebe tried to back out of the tent quickly, but the demon was faster than she had anticipated. He bounded over the elephant in a flash, pouncing on Phoebe with the speed and precision of a tiger.

Reacting purely on instinct, Phoebe made a roundhouse kick to the demon's chest. The demon stumbled back a half step, but was otherwise unaffected.

The Bestiari hissed at Phoebe. She knew that he had the defensive abilities of a wide selection of animals and it occurred to her that he might also be poisonous.

She had no intention of finding out.

Phoebe let loose with a barrage of fists hitting

the demon with every move she had learned in her martial arts training. She could have been hitting him with a fly swatter, for all the good she was doing. Apparently the demon realized this, too, as he let loose with a shrill laugh much like a hyena's.

Knowing she was fighting a losing battle, Phoebe drew back from the demon, looking for an avenue of escape. She didn't want to turn her back on him, but she knew that backing away wouldn't give her the speed she needed to get out of his path.

As Phoebe considered her options, the Bestiari Demon lashed out at her with one hand, hitting her squarely in the chest and sending her flying backward out of the tent.

"Cotton candy!" she heard Paige yell from behind her. A half-second later she landed in a pile of plastic bags filled with the pink and blue sugary confection.

"Are you okay?" Piper asked as she and Paige hurried to Phoebe's side.

"Yeah," Phoebe said as she pulled herself up. Several of the bags of candy had burst on impact, and strands of cotton candy were cling-ing to her clothes. "You couldn't have orbed me onto a pile of foam pillows?"

Paige helped her sister remove the candy from her hair. "I work with what's available," she said, pointing to a cotton candy stand nearby. "Next time you go flying in the air, try to do it near an air mattress and we won't have this kind of problem."

"I'm guessing you found the demon," Piper said.

"It's the clown," Phoebe replied. She was surprised—and relieved—that he hadn't followed her out of the tent. "The stupid clown that's been messing with us all day."

"We know," Piper said. "We found the tape. He gave quite a performance. And here we were thinking it was Puck all along."

"It serves us right for judging a demon by his cover," Paige said.

"He's almost done draining Tasha's life," Phoebe said as she hurried back toward the tent.

"Phoebe wait," Piper said as she and Paige followed. "We need to vanquish him together."

The Charmed Ones locked hands and slowly entered the tent.

"I came up with the spell earlier," Paige said. "Repeat after—"

"Forget it," Piper said as her eyes adjusted to the dark tent. "He's gone."

Piper was right: Tasha was the only living being in the tent. The space was large and empty, save the untouched hay bales shoved in the corner. Phoebe tentatively checked behind them, but the space was empty. There was nowhere for the demon to hide. He had vanished.

"But how?" Phoebe asked. "We were right outside."

"There's your answer," Paige said, pointing to a large tear in the back of the tent.

"Tasha!" Phoebe said, hurrying to the elephant's side.

The demon hadn't been able to finish the job. Phoebe could tell Tasha was still alive by the rapid rise and fall of her torso. Her breathing was still labored, and she looked even worse than she had before. It was clear that if Phoebe hadn't gone into the tent before she found her sisters, Tasha would already be gone.

"I don't think the demon has killed in the daytime before," Phoebe said. "Why now?"

"Maybe he knew we were onto him," Paige said.

"What the hell are you doing in here . . . again?" Lane demanded as she came into the tent. She was dressed in her flashy circus costume—a silver sequined jacket over a shiny black bodysuit. But she didn't look like a jovial circus performer. "This area is under quarantine. No one's supposed to be here."

"There's no time to explain," Phoebe said. "Did you see a clown around here?"

"You're kidding, right?" Lane asked. "You do realize this is a circus."

"Tommy," Phoebe said. "Have you seen Tommy the clown?"

"Tommy?" Piper mumbled. "The demon's name is Tommy?"

"Not since the show started," Lane replied.

"No. He didn't . . . never mind," Phoebe said as she grabbed her sisters and hurried out of the tent. "We don't have time for this."

"I'm calling security," Lane called after them.

"Good!" Paige yelled back. "Get the whole force out here, if you can."

The three sisters stopped outside the tent, scanning the area for the Bestiari Demon.

"We've got to find that clown before the others come out of the arena," Paige said. "Or else it will be like looking for a needle in a clown stack."

"Too late," Piper said, pointing to the arena's side exit.

A dozen clowns were streaming out of the Cow Palace and heading right for the Charmed Ones.

Chapter 18

"Is it just me, or are those clowns headed straight for us?" Phoebe asked as she instinctively took a step back.

"It's a stampede," Paige said dryly.

Piper found it unsettling to watch as a swarm of clowns converged on her and her sisters. She wasn't sure why they were running directly toward the three of them. She checked her watch. They couldn't possibly be done already—the show was only half over. And this seemed like an odd way to spend their downtime between appearances onstage.

The only explanation for the mass exodus was that Tommy the demon clown had called on his unsuspecting cohorts to protect him. Little did the clowns know they'd be helping the person who was responsible for killing their beloved animal coworkers, closing down the circus, and leaving them all without a job.

"This is not good," Paige said. "How are we

going to find the demon among all these clowns? They're practically identical."

"One red nose at a time," Piper said, bracing herself as the group crowded around them.

Piper wasn't certain that the Bestiari Demon was hiding among the gaggle of clowns. But he would have blended right in. It would be easy for him to separate the Charmed Ones and take them out one by one while his cronies thought they were just playing some kind of game. It was almost the kind of joke befitting Puck, though the endgame was far more sinister.

"Stick together," Piper yelled as she tried to reach for her sisters' hands.

Instead of Phoebe's hand, Piper felt something cold and wet against her palm. She looked down to find that she was holding what looked to be a dead fish. She dropped it quickly. Even though she was pretty sure it wasn't a real fish, it still left a slimy residue on her hand. She tried to wipe it off on the nearest clown and wound up pulling off the guy's tear-away shirt, revealing a chest that had a huge face painted on it. The clown screamed in fake embarrassment, waving his hands wildly in Piper's face so she couldn't see.

Piper managed to turn away from him in time to see Paige being pulled away from the crowd by a clown wearing a hat that rose five feet into the air. Paige was struggling to get away from the clown, but it was clear that she didn't want to hurt the guy. Her struggle proved useless as she was quickly trapped in the center of a ring of five clowns holding hands and skipping around her.

For a moment it looked like Paige was enjoying herself. Piper figured her sister was just playing along so she could get a good look at the clowns and try to identify the Bestiari Demon. Paige was even bouncing on the balls of her feet in rhythm with the clowns as she got a good look at each of their faces.

Piper tried to do the same with the clowns around her, but it was hard to get a positive ID on any of them because they kept moving around wildly. Two of the clowns were obviously female, which made them easy to cross off the list. The third clown was a man dressed up as a woman. He was harder to identify because of his extra layers of padding and stylized makeup. It was especially difficult to see the clowns' faces when they started tossing streamers at Piper like it was New Year's Eve.

Of course, all the demon had to do was remove his makeup and then no one would be able to identify him at all, Piper thought.

As Piper worked to free herself from the streamers, she saw that Phoebe was trapped between the giant legs of several stilt-walking clowns who had joined their normal-size brethren. All it would have taken for Phoebe to escape was a few swift kicks to the stilts, but

Phoebe would never hurt the innocent clowns like that. It wasn't their fault they had been tricked into covering for a demon.

Between the clowns, the streamers, and the crazy honking and whistling sounds being made around her, it was like Piper was in the middle ring of the circus, with all the acts performing at once. The clowns were having a grand old time, but Piper could no longer make heads or tails of her surroundings, much less notice if the Bestiari Demon was among the crowd. She threw up her hands and froze the group of clowns.

"Thank you," Phoebe said with relief as she slipped between the legs of a clown on stilts and helped Piper free herself from the streamers.

"I don't know . . . that was kind of fun," Paige said as she ducked under two clasped hands in the ring of clowns.

Her sisters did not share in her enjoyment.

"Or it would have been," Paige continued meekly, "if the life of a defenseless animal didn't hang in the balance."

Piper decided not to comment on Paige's statement. "I doubt the Bestiari Demon—"

"Tommy," Phoebe said.

"I refuse to call the demon 'Tommy,'" Piper said. "Anyway, I doubt he's part of this crowd, but let's give them the once-over."

Piper and Paige evaluated the nearest demons. Even though they had only seen the demon clown briefly throughout the day, they had enough of an idea of his body type to know that he wasn't among their comic attackers. Phoebe levitated herself to check out the clowns on stilts and arrived at the same conclusion.

"Now what?" Paige asked.

"Now we get out of here before the clowns unfreeze," Piper said.

"But won't they think it's weird that we just disappeared?" Paige asked.

"There's so much going on that they'll probably think we managed to sneak away in the confusion," Phoebe said. "Either way, I'm not getting back in the middle of that insanity."

"Me neither," Piper said as she led her sisters over to the row of trailers away from the group of entertainers. Looking back at the frozen tableau of wild colors and painted faces, Piper was a little freaked out by the sight. There was just something eerie about the scene. Piper could understand why some people suffered a severe phobia of clowns.

Once she and her sisters were far enough away from the group, Piper quickly unfroze the clowns and watched as they continued their routine. They were all so involved in what they were doing that it took them a moment to realize the women had disappeared. Once they did, they began stretching out their already exaggerated expressions.

For the first time since the clown encounter had begun, Piper actually felt like laughing.

Now that they had lost their audience, the clowns came down a bit from their zany act and slowly started to head back toward the arena. Piper heaved a sigh of relief, but it was premature. One of the female clowns had turned back in their direction and noticed the Charmed Ones poking their heads out from behind the trailer.

A maliciously wide grin spread across the clown's face as Piper silently willed the woman to leave them alone. Piper knew that she couldn't freeze time and disappear again. That would be too hard to explain. She could only watch as the clown blew her whistle and the rest of the group stopped walking. When they turned to see what the noise was about, the whistle-blower pointed in the direction of the Charmed Ones.

"I suggest we exit, stage right," Paige said as she and her sisters took off running.

Piper, Phoebe, and Paige hurried down the corridors between the trailers with the clowns hot on their trail.

It seemed unlikely that they would go to the trouble of an actual search just to continue playing games with their victims. However, Piper knew if she was in that situation and had come across three women with the ability to disappear so quickly, she would have wanted to find the women, if only to see if they could do it again.

The Charmed Ones turned a corner and were surprised to find that the clowns had apparently split up. Another contingent was heading straight for them from the opposite direction.

"Follow me!" Piper yelled as she quickly ducked between two trailers.

Once she saw that her sisters were with her, she turned to Paige. "Orb us to the media trailer."

She knew they were taking a risk—the media trailer might not be empty—but it was the first place she had thought of. Thankfully, when they rematerialized, they found that they were alone in the small room. Piper and her sisters each breathed a sigh of relief.

"Let's wait a few minutes to let the clowns settle down," Piper said. "They have to go back in the arena soon. I can't imagine they're done performing."

She peeked out a small window along the trailer's south wall. She didn't see any clowns outside, but she knew they were out there.

I can't believe we're being hunted by circus clowns, she thought.

"We should be out searching for the Bestiari Demon," Paige said, venting her frustration. The three of them were well aware that he had the upper hand at the moment. "We—and Tasha— are running out of time."

"Wait a minute," Phoebe said. "The demon doesn't have much time either."

"Where are you going with this?" Paige asked. Phoebe was clearly trying to figure something out.

"We've been going about this the wrong way," Phoebe finally said. "Tasha's still alive, right? So, the demon is going to have to go back and finish the job. And he can't fully absorb her essence until she's dead. All we have to do is wait with Tasha, and the demon will come to us."

Piper thought back to her list of things she was supposed to do today. Babysitting a dying elephant was not on it. She always found it amazing how her plans for a day could totally spiral out of control.

"This is definitely not how I had intended to spend my afternoon."

Chapter 19

"Wouldn't it be funny if Tasha was really Puck in disguise, and all this was just an incredibly well-orchestrated prank?" Paige wondered aloud as they walked back to Tasha's tent. "You know, like he's filming us for some otherworldly reality show."

Her sisters just glared at her.

"Okay, well, not funny ha-ha, but . . . never mind," Paige mumbled.

The Charmed Ones had waited almost ten minutes in the media trailer for the clowns to disperse. They were thankful that Reed hadn't come into the trailer while they were hiding. It would have been hard to explain that they were hiding from a gang of rogue clowns. Once they determined that enough time had passed, the Charmed Ones eventually left the trailer.

Phoebe led the way as they hurried back to Tasha's tent. After they had worked their way to the edge of the mobile units, they stopped behind the last trailer in the row. Someone had finally gotten around to posting a guard outside Tasha's tent to enforce the quarantine. Phoebe suspected that Lane had given someone hell for abandoning his post earlier. The bald-headed guard had his back to the tent and was keeping a well-trained eye out for any trespassers.

Piper raised her hands, freezing time.

"Well, that was easy," Paige said, sounding a little disappointed.

Unfortunately, her disappointment was premature. As soon as the Charmed Ones stepped out from behind the trailer, Phoebe noticed something unexpected. "Um . . . the guard is not frozen," she said.

She was right. The guard continued to scan the area intently. It only took a second for him to spot the Charmed Ones.

They tried unsuccessfully to look nonchalant.

"Either my power's on the fritz," Piper said, nodding to the unfrozen guard, "or that's an Upper-Level Demon too."

"I guess now would be a good time to mention the Bestiari is an Upper-Level Demon?" Paige asked meekly.

"Yeah," Piper said. "Actually, it would have been better to know that a little bit earlier. What's with you? That's an amateur mistake."

"Sorry," Paige said weakly.

"Phoebe, I thought you said this guy was always in his clown makeup," Piper said.

"That's what I was told," Phoebe replied.

Not surprisingly, the demon looked much more threatening when his head wasn't painted red and white. His muscular body—hidden under the baggy clown clothes—was now bursting out of the security uniform, which was a few sizes too small. He seemed far more imposing now than when he was in the clown suit.

It was a standoff.

"We're too late," Paige said. "He must have finished Tasha off by now."

"Then why would he stick around?" Piper asked.

"Tasha's still alive," Phoebe said. "He's using her as bait, just like we were planning to do."

"That's ironic," Paige said.

"Maybe he doesn't know that we know it's him," Piper said. Though she doubted that it really mattered since they had been staring at him for so long.

The Bestiari Demon's lip curled into a snarl as he kept a close watch on the Charmed Ones.

"He knows," Piper said.

Without warning, the Bestiari charged toward them like a racing stallion.

The demon slammed into Paige, knocking her ten feet backward. She crashed into the wall of the veterinarian's trailer.

Phoebe planted a roundhouse kick at the demon's jaw. He barely faltered. Instead, he lashed out at Piper, sending her sprawling to the ground.

The demon then turned toward Phoebe. His eyes burned red with hunger. Paige hadn't mentioned anything about the demon draining the life-essence from humans—or witches—but it looked like he was ready to try something new.

Phoebe, however, was not up for the experiment, and she did the first thing that came to mind.

She ran.

Phoebe knew from experience that she did not have the strength to take on a demon with the power of a horse, a tiger, and countless other animals. All she could do was try to outrun the Bestiari for the time being while her sisters worked on a plan of attack. She only hoped that the demon would follow her.

He didn't let her down.

Phoebe could hear the demon behind her, closing the distance quickly. She felt his hand brush against her hair.

Phoebe immediately dropped to the ground, rolling under the trailer and popping up on the other side. The move must have caught the demon off-guard, because he didn't immediately follow. Phoebe used the distraction to her advantage, and put as many mobile units between herself and the demon as possible.

She quickly dashed behind the nearest row of trailers, hiding between a pair of double-wides that must have served as the main offices. She frantically looked around for a place to hide.

She ran up to the door to one of the offices, but found that it was locked. She considered banging on it, but she didn't want anyone who might be inside to be hurt by the demon. Phoebe could hear her pursuer's footsteps as he approached. He was almost on top of her.

She ran down the small staircase, hoping to make a silent escape when she realized she had literally backed herself into a corner. The two double-wides intersected with a third trailer, ending the corridor in a U. With nowhere to turn, the only place she could go was up.

Phoebe concentrated on the extreme feeling of duress she was under and used it to fuel her power of levitation just in time. She watched from above as the demon came around the corner and stopped only a few inches below her feet. Phoebe held her breath, not wanting to alert the demon to her presence above him.

The ruse worked. Unaware that Phoebe was hovering above his head, the demon turned and went back through the maze of trailers to search for her.

Phoebe managed to pull herself over to the roof of the double-wide. She watched as the demon headed away from her in his security uniform. Paige wondered what had happened to the real security guard, and suspected that the demon had already taken one human victim today. She feared that she and her sisters might be next.

She turned to see if she could find Tasha's tent from her position. It wasn't hard to spot. She also saw that both her sisters had gotten back to their feet. They looked shaken, but otherwise fine. Phoebe waved her hands above her head, trying to get their attention.

Even from a distance, Phoebe could see the relief on Piper's and Paige's faces when they saw that she was all right. Since it was safer to travel by rooftop, Phoebe hurried back to Tasha's tent, jumping from trailer to trailer to avoid being seen by the demon. Conveniently, the trailers were laid out in such a way that she didn't have to touch the ground once en route to the tent.

Phoebe spotted the Bestiari Demon again before she reached her destination. He was still heading in the wrong direction, so there would be plenty of time for the Charmed Ones to regroup.

It didn't take long for Phoebe to reach Tasha's tent. On the way there she had seen her sisters go inside, so she knew that they were waiting for her.

She checked the area to make sure it was demon- and clown-free before she climbed down from the final trailer. As she descended, she noticed that it was the veterinarian's trailer.

Breathless, she hurried into the tent. She could tell that they didn't have much time. Phoebe wasn't an expert in animal medicine, but it was clear that Tasha was suffering even worse than when they had last seen her. The demon had started his final drain, and the elephant looked like she was in the last stages of life. All it would take was a single touch from the Bestiari Demon and Tasha would be gone.

"We are going to make this demon pay," Paige said angrily as Phoebe joined her sisters beside Tasha. It was heartbreaking to see such a strong creature look so weak. Phoebe could totally understand Paige's rage. She felt the same way.

They knew that the Bestiari Demon would be back soon. He needed to finish the job in order to tap into Tasha's power. Phoebe, Piper, and Paige had no intention of allowing that to happen.

The Charmed Ones moved into position, placing themselves between Tasha and the door. At the same time, Phoebe kept looking back at the tear in the tent the Bestiari had made earlier. They did not want to be caught by surprise.

As they waited, Paige told them the spell she had come up with earlier.

"You've got to be kidding," Piper said upon hearing the words. They had certainly heard worse spells over the years, but this one definitely wasn't going to win any awards for creative writing.

"Hey, give a girl a break," Paige said. "I haven't been doing this as long as you two."

"It's not that bad," Phoebe said. "Just . . . you know . . . the 'strong and hairy' part? That could use a polish."

"I'll get right on it after we save Tasha's life," Paige said.

The three sisters lined up side by side, with Paige in the center, Piper on her left, and Phoebe on her right. All they had to do was wait for the Bestiari Demon to arrive.

They didn't have to wait long.

The Bestiari came bursting into the entrance. He paused for a moment when he saw the Charmed Ones, then continued, crossing the distance between them in a flash.

Piper threw her hands up, attempting to blow up the demon. None of them expected the move to work, but it was somewhat successful. The Bestiari was knocked backward for a moment, which gave them the opportunity they needed.

The Charmed Ones clasped hands and chanted the spell:

> To save the creatures in this realm,
> From powers that can overwhelm.
> For all animals strong and hairy,
> Rid us of this Bestiari.

Phoebe felt Paige's hand tighten around her own. An odd sensation passed between the two sisters as the spell took effect. It was unlike anything Phoebe had ever felt before while casting a Power of Three spell. It was like her magic was being drained out of her body.

The Bestiari stumbled backward, but did not go down.

Phoebe felt her power continue to drain. It was almost as if the Bestiari Demon was feeding off them, but that couldn't be possible. It seemed like he wasn't capable of anything at the moment but struggling to stay alive.

The demon let out an earsplitting scream. It was a horrible noise, like the roar of a tiger, the braying of a horse, and dozens of other growls, screeches, and howls sounding all at once.

But the demon still did not go down.

Phoebe felt her magic being pulled out of her body. Pain shot through her entire being. She wanted to let go of Paige's hand, fall to the ground, and give up.

"What's happening?" she yelled, straining to be heard over the demon's wails.

"I don't know!" Piper yelled back.

Paige remained silent. She was focused on the demon.

Phoebe held fast to her sister. She knew she could not give up. She was beginning to see that the spell was working.

"Tommy, can you hear us?" Paige asked with a smirk.

Phoebe wondered how her sister had the energy to banter.

The demon's howls grew quieter. There was no strength left in his voice. He fell to his knees, but he still managed to stay upright. Phoebe saw him struggling as she felt the last of her energy draining from her body.

Finally, the demon toppled to the ground. His body burst into flames.

Phoebe and Piper immediately fell over as well, completely exhausted.

Paige had managed to stay on her feet, but she looked worn out as well.

It was the most intense Power of Three spell they had ever chanted.

As the smoke cleared, Phoebe heard the soft sound of a trumpet and she knew that it had been a success. Tasha would be fine.

"Whoa," Paige said as she teetered on her feet. "That was powerful."

"You can say that again," Phoebe agreed.

"I didn't know the spell was going to take so much energy," Piper said as she stood up. "It was like all my magic was draining from my body."

"Yeah," Paige agreed. "That part wasn't in the Book of Shadows. I'm starting to think it's not exactly the most informative reference guide available."

Phoebe couldn't argue. Aside from the fact that she agreed with the sentiment, she would have been too tired to say anything if she hadn't.

After about a minute, Phoebe managed to get back to her feet. She could feel her strength and her energy coming back to her slowly. It had been one hell of a fight.

As the Charmed Ones took stock of their health, they noticed a large shadow falling over them. Turning, they saw that Tasha was back on her feet, already looking one hundred percent better.

The elephant let out a deafening trumpet sound that was clearly her way of saying, "thank you."

Chapter 20

"Leo?" Piper called out softly as the Charmed Ones orbed into the living room of Halliwell Manor. She didn't want to wake her son if he was napping.

There was no response. Piper picked up the baby monitor, but she didn't hear anything.

"Maybe he's upstairs with Wyatt?" Phoebe suggested.

"They could both be napping," Paige added. "Maybe you should let them sleep. Spending a morning with the Elders is probably exhausting. Imagine how much work it is to keep from being bored to death. Oh wait, technically, they're already dead."

"It's no more exhausting than what we've just been through," Piper said.

After they had dealt with the demon and regained enough strength to get back on their feet, she, Phoebe, and Paige had quickly left Tasha's tent through the tear in the back wall. They had figured it wouldn't be long before someone came to investigate the trumpet noise that Tasha had made. It was pure luck that no one had come to investigate while the Bestiari was howling his life away. *Then again, no one in their right mind would want to see what could make a sound so hideous*, Piper thought.

Before they had orbed home, the three sisters had gone back to Reed's trailer to pick up the press release that Reed had promised earlier. Reed seemed more impressed than intimidated that Phoebe had two assistants, and after sitting through some more innocent flirtation between Phoebe and Reed, they all celebrated when the veterinarian came bursting into the trailer to report that Tasha was back on her feet and looking much better.

Reed had happily torn up his latest press release while Phoebe put on a show, lamenting the fact that she had lost her story. Piper couldn't help but think that her sister wasn't entirely acting. It was possible that Phoebe had caught the journalism bug. Although it was more likely that it was just a passing fancy. Piper knew Phoebe loved writing her advice column, and she doubted that anything would take the place of that job anytime soon.

"Now that we're done at the circus, Leo can go back to his retreat with the Elders," Piper said as she moved toward the stairs. "Maybe if he goes back, they'll be less upset with him for cutting out in the first place."

"The Elders are a rather sensitive lot, aren't they?" Paige said.

Piper looked back at her sister. *A rather sensitive lot?*

Paige had made several odd comments throughout the day. Piper had attributed them to the stress of the situation, but now she wasn't so sure. Paige had also been relying on inappropriately timed humor way more than usual.

Piper pushed her suspicions out of her mind as they reached the nursery. Wyatt was lying in his crib. He was awake and giggling, but his father was nowhere to be found.

"Hey honey," she said as she reached out to rub his soft hair. "Someone's in a good mood. Where's Daddy?"

"Piper," Phoebe said as she came in behind her sister. Piper immediately sensed something was wrong by her sister's tone. "Why does the nursery look like a petting zoo?"

Piper turned away from the crib to see several birds and small animals sitting quietly on the changing table. At first she had thought they were stuffed animals since they were totally still. They were staring intently at the baby, but not in a threatening way. It was almost like they were keeping watch over him.

"That's a good question," she said, turning to Paige. "It didn't look this way when I left Wyatt with Leo. Although I'm not entirely sure I *did* leave Wyatt with Leo. Why don't *you* fill us in on what we're missing . . . Puck?"

"Puck?" Paige said. "Hello! I'm Paige. Your half-sister? I realize we haven't known each other that long, but I thought you would recognize me by now."

"You can drop the act," Phoebe said, moving beside Piper so they were between "Paige" and the baby. She looked at Piper. "I'm guessing we both figured it out at the same time?"

Piper nodded. "When we vanquished the demon, I could feel my magic draining from me," Piper said. "But the Bestiari Demon wasn't the one doing it. All my energy was going straight into my dear sister beside me."

"Our magic doesn't work that way," Phoebe added. "It doesn't filter through one of us."

"Of course, we should have figured it out earlier," Piper said. "Paige has been a little off all day. What with the one-liners and the intense need to defend almost everything Puck said and did."

"Is it so wrong to want to give the guy the benefit of the doubt?" Paige asked, though there was a slight giggle in her voice. She seemed to be enjoying this, rather than experiencing concern at not being recognized by her own family.

"And Paige never seemed to be around when Puck dropped in," Phoebe added. "She burst into orbs when he came to meet us."

"Will you please stop referring to me in the third person?" Paige said. "It's a little annoying."

"But in the media trailer, *Paige* was with us while Puck was on the TV screen," Piper added. "That time, Paige was surprisingly silent, and we had all those questions for Puck."

"Okay," Paige said, holding up her hands in surrender. "You got me."

Paige's face broke into an inhumanly large grin as her body grew about half a foot taller. Her hair began to pale until it went totally bleached blond, and then white. Her feminine features twisted and changed into a more masculine—though slightly androgynous—appearance. And finally, her outfit changed into a flashy loud suit.

"Boy, you gals are better than I gave you credit for," Puck said with glee. "I didn't think you'd figure out that last part on your own."

"Well, you had done your homework. You knew all about us," Phoebe said.

"Did you think you were dealing with an amateur?" Puck asked, mildly offended. "Did you think my true reflection was going to show up in a mirror? Or that I was going to dip into some coffee ice cream even though Paige doesn't like that flavor? I'm Puck. I was born *waaaaay* before yesterday."

"Where's Paige?" Piper asked. She hoped her sister was somewhere in the forest, setting up camp and enjoying an afternoon of meditation. But somehow Piper didn't trust Puck to have let Paige get off so easily.

"Don't you want to know why I enacted this incredibly intricate charade?" Puck asked. "Where's your sense of curiosity? What happened to that wonderful investigative spirit we tapped into earlier?"

"We'd rather know what you've done with our sister," Phoebe said.

"All in good time," Puck said. "All in good time. But first, you deserve a reward."

"Reward?" Phoebe asked.

"For helping me out," Puck said. "Didn't I mention there would be a prize earlier? I'm almost certain I did. Oh, and don't worry about that personal gain nonsense. There are always ways around that."

"I'll tell you what," Piper said. "Why don't you make Paige our reward and bring her to us."

"You and your one-track mind." Puck laughed. "Anyway, I have to admit you were such good sports. I truly couldn't have done it without you. You see, that particular Bestiari has been plaguing me for years. As strong as I am, I was no match for the pure strength of the animal spirits he had in reserve. Therefore, I needed the help of a pair of powerful witches—two of the most powerful witches in the world—to work with me."

"Why didn't you just ask for our help?" Piper asked.

"Well, where's the fun in that?" Puck said, as if that explained everything. "Besides, how else was I going to decide whether you were friend or foe? I did say this was a test, after all."

"I'd hate to know what would have happened if we had failed," Phoebe said sarcastically.

"Me too," Puck said darkly. Then he quickly returned to his perky self. "But you didn't. Aren't you proud of yourselves?"

"Why didn't you just tell us about the demon and what he looked like?" Piper asked. She wasn't ready to let this go. Puck *had* been playing games with them all day. They could have just gone in, taken care of the Bestiari, and gone back home, all before Wyatt's naptime.

"I wanted to see you in action," Puck replied. "I wanted to observe the Charmed Ones in their supernatural setting. Besides, I did give you clues along the way—like when I told you to stop *clowning* around."

"Yeah, that was a big help," Phoebe said. "I think we did pretty well on our own, thank you very much."

"And imagine my surprise," Puck said. "How would I have seen that you could prove yourselves so handily with the whole investigation if I had just told you everything you needed to know. I thought you had some kind of demon-divining rod that would start pointing every time you were near a demon."

"That would be helpful," Piper said.

"I just have one question," Phoebe said.

"Actually, the two of you have had about a

dozen questions, so far," Puck said, "but let's not quibble. What would you like to know?"

"If Tommy the clown had been with the circus for years, why didn't he kill any of those animals before?" Phoebe asked. "And why did he stop going to the zoos to feed?"

"Um . . . that's two questions," Puck said.

Piper was starting to get annoyed. "Puck," she said threateningly.

"Did you ever hear the phrase 'you don't pass excrement where you eat'?"

"I'm familiar with it," Phoebe said.

"Same thing," Puck explained. "The circus provided cover for the demon's travels, and the animals were there if he needed them. But you saw how everyone was on alert after only two of the animals had taken ill. How long could he have gone on if he took an animal a month from the circus?"

"But he stopped attacking zoo animals," Piper said, reminding him of the second part of Phoebe's question.

"Okay, well, as we've already established, I'm one bad demon," Puck said. "But my power only goes so far. Since I couldn't stop the demon permanently, I cut him off from his source of prey. I found this nifty little spell that would keep the Bestiari from entering any place where I'd cast the spell."

Piper had suspected that it hadn't been the Bestiari's idea to stop feeding at the zoo. "But why—"

"Why didn't I cast the spell on the circus?" Puck said, finishing her question. "Because it only works on permanent locations. It doesn't work on a moving circus, or an arena that brings in different events every week."

"So you basically forced him to start killing the circus animals," Piper said.

"I admit there was a flaw in my plan," Puck said with genuine sadness. "But I knew that the circus was coming to San Francisco, home of the legendary Charmed Ones."

"Stop it, we're blushing," Piper said, dryly.

"Oh you," Puck said with a wave. "And now, I must take my leave." He cleared his throat and held out his arms to Piper and Phoebe. "Give me your hands, if we be friends, and Robin shall restore amends."

Piper and Phoebe both crossed their arms.

"Fine," Puck said. "Be that way."

With that, he disappeared, leaving an echoing "Ho, ho, ho" behind him.

"Hey!" Piper yelled into the air. "Where's our—"

Suddenly, Paige orbed into the room. There were twigs in her hair, a tear in her shirt, and her pants were caked with mud. She looked tired and disheveled, and surprised that she was back at home.

"Are you okay?" Piper asked.

"I am having one heck of a day," Paige said as she collapsed into the rocking chair that sat in a corner of the nursery. "I've been stuck wandering through the forest for hours. I'm dirty, I'm exhausted . . . and some creep stole my backpack and tossed it in the river."

"We heard," Phoebe mumbled.

Paige didn't notice and continued with her rant. "Then, I couldn't orb home. I've been trying and trying, but nothing happened. Then, all of a sudden, I wasn't even thinking about home, and here I am. I think it has something to do with this flower the guy stuck in my hair. I haven't been able to get it—"

The flower fell to the ground.

"Okay," Paige said, finally stopping for a breath, "what's going on?"

"It's a long story," Phoebe said. "But we've dealt with the creep."

"For now," Piper quickly added. "I bet we'll be seeing him again."

Just then, a small rectangular box tied with a bow appeared on the changing table, right in front of the raccoon.

"Why is there—" Paige started to ask as she saw the row of animals. "Never mind. I don't want to know."

"Shoo," Piper said to the animals, but instead of running away, they disappeared.

Piper picked up the box, slipped off the bow, and opened the lid. She gave a defeated little laugh when she saw what was inside.

"What is it?" Phoebe asked.

"Our reward," Piper said as she removed three slips of paper and showed them to her sisters. "Tickets to the Fletcher Family Circus."

"Some prize," Phoebe said. "I still have the comp tickets that Reed gave me."

Epilogue

Dr. Jordan Kahn took a leisurely stroll through the parking lot he called home. It had been a long month, and he was exceedingly tired. A man his age shouldn't have to put up with the crazy things that went on at a circus. He should be relaxing on a beach year round.

Oh, who am I kidding? He thought. *I hate sand in my shorts.*

Jordan laughed a dry laugh.

Since the afternoon performance was still wrapping up, he had no one to celebrate with. He had wanted to hoist a few with Reed, but the poor, overworked kid was too focused on trying to write a press release announcing that an elephant that nobody outside the circus knew was sick in the first place had gotten well. To Reed's disappointment, Jordan couldn't explain how the elephant had been cured.

Just chalk it up to one of those unexplained mysteries, he had told Reed.

Jordan finally reached his trailer. It seemed to be taking him longer and longer to get around these days. At least when he got inside he'd be able to pour himself some whiskey.

The two steps up to the trailer were getting harder to navigate as well. He refused to go in for the knee surgery he knew he should have. He had no use for medical doctors. There were very few maladies he had suffered in his lifetime that he couldn't find a cure for on his own.

Once he'd gotten up the steps, he unlocked the door and ambled inside, silently debating if he would prefer Scotch or Bourbon.

"What the hell happened here?" he muttered as he discovered that his trailer was a complete mess.

"Oh, sorry. That was me," his white-haired friend said as he came out of the back room. "I was just having some fun. I had to challenge the girls a bit. I couldn't let them find those tapes too easily. If you ask me, that Bestiari Demon was far too easy to get rid of."

"You are one strange creature, Puck," Jordan said as he pushed some old magazines off the nearest chair so he could sit down.

"Let me take care of that for you," Puck said. With a snap of his fingers, Puck straightened up the trailer, making it cleaner than Jordan had ever seen it.

"Thank you," Jordan said as he sat. He didn't know why he was thanking the little devil, considering that Puck had been the one to mess up the trailer in the first place.

"I have to say," Jordan continued, "I didn't think those two young ladies would prove to be so darned helpful."

Jordan leaned down and opened the cabinet under the sink. He bypassed both the Scotch and the Bourbon and pulled out a bottle of rum. He set it down on the table beside him.

"You find the most unexpected things when dealing with the magical realm," Puck said as he took a glass from a cabinet and handed it to Jordan.

"You don't have to tell me that," Jordan said. He had found magic to be quite useful over the many years of his life. It had all started back when he had met a young lady friend who'd told him she was a witch. The relationship didn't last, but once he had learned there was magic in the world, he sought it out whenever he could.

Though he wasn't actually magical himself, Jordan had managed to use otherworldly powers to his benefit once in a while. At over 325 years old, he was the oldest living mortal he had ever come across.

Of course, nothing had been more useful to him than the discovery that the mythical creature known as Puck truly existed.

"You've been a great help today, Puck," Jordan said.

"I like to give back to the community every

now and then," Puck said. "You can't always go around misleading travelers in the dark. It gets a little old."

"Many things do, I'm afraid," Jordan said, pouring rum into his glass.

When Jordan had realized that someone at the circus was behind the deaths of various animals across the country, he knew he had to do something. At first he was mad that he hadn't noticed it earlier. But every time the news reported on the deaths at the zoos, the circus had already moved on to the next city.

In hindsight, Jordan realized how foolish he had been not to see that the murderer was Tommy. But they had been friends for so long, he had been totally fooled. If only Puck had told him before today who the demon was. But Puck liked to do things his way, no matter if they made sense or not.

It had been a brilliant stroke of luck the day that Jordan had accidentally stumbled across the spell to summon Puck. Considering the mythical being was widely known for his love of animals, Jordan knew contacting the prankster to ask for help was worth the risk.

Surprisingly, Puck had agreed easily. He even came up with the plan. Jordan only wished they could have found a way to stop the demon without losing any of his dear animals in the process.

"Well, I'd best be going," Puck said.

"You sure you don't want to have a glass?"

Jordan asked, holding up his rum. He hated to drink alone.

"I have things to do," Puck said. He held up a tacky old polyester suit Jordan had held on to since the seventies. As a man of more than three hundred, he had accumulated quite a wardrobe. There were storage facilities all over the world full of his old junk. "I think I'll take this for my fee," Puck said.

"Go right ahead," Jordan said, happy to be rid of the thing.

"It was a pleasure doing business with you," Puck said. After a bow and a salute, Puck disappeared with Jordan's suit.

"Here's to you, Puck," Jordan said as he raised his glass. He smiled as he tipped it back, knowing that he had truly earned this drink. The liquid felt good as it slipped past his lips, but he nearly choked on it as it rolled over his tongue and down his throat.

Jordan spit out what was left in his mouth. "Puck!" he screamed into the air.

The merry little prankster had replaced his liquor with apple juice.

"Ho, ho, ho!"

About the Author

Paul Ruditis has written and contributed to books based on such notable TV series as Buffy the Vampire Slayer, Angel, Star Trek, Queer as Folk, and The West Wing. He is the author of Charmed: The Brewing Storm and co-author of The Book of Three, the official episode guide for the series. He lives in Burbank, California.